CROS[S]

'Which one of you three young ladies would be Holly Adams?' asked the shopkeeper.

'That's me,' said Holly. 'But how . . .?'

The man opened a drawer and drew out a folded sheet of paper. 'I was asked to give this to you.'

Holly stared at the piece of paper. 'I don't understand,' she said.

'A young gentleman by the name of Jamie gave it to me,' said the shopkeeper. 'He was in here about half an hour ago with another young gentleman.'

'Jamie!' gasped Holly.

'He beat us to it!' said Tracy. 'The little beast!'

Holly unfolded the sheet of paper. Belinda and Tracy leaned over her shoulders. It was written in Jamie's spidery handwriting.

The Mystery Club is rubbish! they read. *We got here first*!

The Mystery Club series

Crossed Lines
The Mystery Club 10

Fiona Kelly

Hodder
Children's
Books

a division of Hodder Headline plc

Special thanks to Allan Frewin Jones

Copyright © by Ben M. Baglio 1994
Created by Ben M. Baglio
London W6 0HE
First published in Great Britain in 1994 by Knight Books

10 9 8 7 6 5 4 3 2

A Catalogue record for this book is
available from the British Library

ISBN 0 340 60726 2

Typeset by Hewer Text Composition Services, Edinburgh
Printed and bound in Great Britain by
Cox & Wyman Ltd, Reading, Berkshire

Hodder Children's Books
a division of Hodder Headline plc
338 Euston Road
London NW1 3BH

1 *The voice on the telephone*

Oh, no! *Now* what? Holly Adams looked up from her book at the sound of the doorbell. She was beginning to suspect there was a conspiracy to try and disturb her as much as possible.

It had taken her most of the morning to read just a couple of chapters of her new P. J. Benson mystery book, what with all the workmen clumping about hammering and drilling and shouting instructions to one another.

With a sigh, Holly clambered off her bed, tucking her short brown hair behind her ears as she slapped the book down on the duvet and headed downstairs.

Ever since Holly and her family had come up from London to live in the little Yorkshire town of Willow Dale, they had been sharing the four-bedroomed cottage with a steady stream of workmen. Sometimes it seemed as if the renovations to their home would never be finished. Especially days like today, with Holly left on her own by her parents to keep an eye on the house.

Holly had quickly discovered that house-sitting and reading didn't mix.

It didn't help, either, that the electricity had been temporarily turned off and that all the outside doors were wide open to allow the workmen in and out.

A chilling breeze was cutting its way along the hall as Holly came down the stairs.

This is a really brilliant time of year to turn the house into an open-plan igloo! she thought.

Throughout the school holiday, wave after wave of freezing north-easterly air had been pouring down across the country. Snow had been threatened. Further north there were reports of snowdrifts two metres deep, but as yet Willow Dale had been spared all but a few flurries.

Holly was fond of snow. She was looking forward to seeing the rolling Yorkshire hills transformed by a blanket of pure white. But as she came shivering down the stairs, she couldn't help wishing that it was summer.

The front door was wide open. A man in a heavy brown coat was standing on the doorstep. He looked to be in his thirties, with red-framed spectacles and a chubby face, his pale hair combed in an attempt to conceal his balding head. He held a clipboard across one forearm and as Holly approached he was busy gnawing at the end of a ballpoint pen.

'Mr Adams?' asked the man.

Holly smiled. 'No. *Miss* Adams,' she said. 'My dad's out. Did you want to speak to him?'

The man extended a plump hand. 'Tony Blake,' he said. Holly shook his soft, warm hand. 'From Gardener, Preston and Blake. The surveyors. Your father was expecting me.'

'Oh, yes.' Holly remembered. Along with countless other instructions, Mr Adams had told her to expect a man from the company of surveyors who were overseeing the work on the house. 'My dad won't be back for a while,' she told Tony Blake. 'He said you could have a look round, if you like, and he'll talk to you as soon as he arrives home. Is that OK?'

Tony Blake nodded. 'Yes, that's fine.'

'Do you want me to show you around?' asked Holly.

'No, no. That's all right,' said Tony Blake. 'I'll find my own way around.' He smiled. 'Don't worry about me. You carry on doing whatever you were doing.'

A chance would be a fine thing, thought Holly, as a burst of hammering came echoing up from the cellar. She heard the deep bark of a dog from somewhere outside.

Tony Blake looked over his shoulder towards a small white van parked at the kerb. Holly saw a long muzzle poking out through the misted-up and slightly opened window.

'I always bring Luther with me,' explained Tony Blake. He shouted down the path. 'Luther! Be quiet. Behave!'

'Will he be OK in there?' asked Holly.

'Yes,' said Tony Blake. 'He'll be fine once he settles down.' He smiled. 'He's better than any car alarm. No one's ever going to steal my van, that's for sure.'

'No,' said Holly. 'I suppose not. Give me a shout if you need anything.'

'Will do,' said Tony Blake.

Holly went back upstairs and picked her book up.

The door opened and a workman's face appeared.

'Oops, sorry,' he said. 'Wrong room.' He closed the door again and she heard him stamp off across the landing.

Holly gave an exasperated laugh. 'It *is*,' she said to herself. 'It's a *conspiracy* to stop me reading this book. Miranda is probably behind it.'

Miranda Hunt had been Holly's closest friend during her childhood years in London. The two of them, along with their friend, Peter Hamilton, had got themselves involved in mysteries long before Holly ever thought of starting up the Mystery Club.

Miranda and Holly exchanged regular letters. One thing they liked to do was to read the first half of a new book, then write to tell each

4

other how they thought the book was going to end. The one whose guess came nearest to how the story actually turned out would be the winner.

Both Holly and Miranda had always loved mystery novels and P. J. Benson was far and away their favourite writer. The shelves in Holly's bedroom were crammed with books, but right then she would have happily sold the lot for just half an hour's peace and quiet with her new one. Much more of this and she'd be getting the letter with Miranda's guesses in it before she'd even read past Chapter One.

She curled up on the bed.

'Chapter Three. The thing in the attic,' she read. 'Juliana Moon crept to the head of the stairs. The attic door stood closed in front of her. The room beyond had been unused, so she had been told, for twenty years. But she had heard noises from up there. She stepped forward and reached for the handle, trembling at the thought of what might lurk within.'

Holly's bedroom door came bursting open, nearly startling her out of her skin.

'Surprise!' yelled Belinda Hayes. 'We've come to keep you company!'

Tracy Foster followed her in. 'We're here to rescue you from boredom,' she said. 'The front door was open so we just came right up. It's

5

freezing out, isn't it? I'm never going to get used to this climate of yours.'

Holly laughed, flinging her book over her shoulder on to the bed. 'I give up,' she said.

Belinda and Tracy were Holly's two best friends at the Winifred Bowen-Davies School. Together the three of them made up the Mystery Club. Holly had formed the club when she had first arrived in Willow Dale, hoping to make friends and meet people who shared her interest in mystery books. But over the past few months they had found little time to *read* about mysteries; real-life mysteries seemed to erupt all around them. It wasn't that they *looked* for adventures. They didn't need to. They seemed to attract mysteries like a magnet!

Belinda pulled her coat off and plumped down on the bed, dressed as usual in her baggy green sweat-shirt and her favourite old jeans. Her eyes sparkled behind her wire-framed spectacles.

'Aren't you pleased to see us?' she asked. 'We thought you'd be bored to death, having to stay in all day with nothing to do.'

'Of course she's pleased to see us,' said Tracy. 'Who wouldn't be?' She put her violin case down. 'I've got a lesson later this afternoon,' she explained. 'So,' she added, 'What are we going to do?'

Holly smiled. It would be difficult, she had often thought, to imagine two people more different than

Belinda and Tracy. Tracy wore smart clothes, her blonde hair neatly styled around her pretty face, whilst Belinda's brown hair looked, as ever, as if it had been caught in a whirlwind. Tracy still had a lot of get-up-and-go from her American childhood. If Belinda had ever had any get-up-and-go, then, as Belinda freely admitted, it had got up and gone some time ago.

Tracy's father was American, but she had been living in Willow Dale with her English mother for three years now, ever since her parents had divorced. Belinda was Yorkshire born and bred, although from looking at her no one would have guessed that she came from one of the wealthiest families in the town.

'We could think up some more ideas for that mystery board game of ours,' said Belinda. It was an idea they had been working on for some time. A game with dice and mystery cards and squares that sometimes gave you clues and sometimes sent you tumbling down a mine shaft or dumped you up to your neck in quicksand.

Holly dragged the prototype board out from under her bed and the three girls sat in a circle on the floor.

They had not been at it for long when the phone rang.

It was Mrs Adams calling from work to remind Holly to give her younger brother, Jamie, a ring to tell him to get home to do his chores. Jamie was notorious for his convenient memory lapses when it came to helping around the house. Somehow housework didn't have the same hold over Jamie as spending the day playing on his friend Philip Owen's computer.

Holly told her mother she'd give him a ring. She was standing in the kitchen trying to find Philip's phone number on the memo board when Belinda and Tracy came down.

'We're a bit peckish,' said Belinda. 'Any chance of a slice of toast or two?'

'*You're* a bit peckish, you mean,' said Tracy. 'I'd just like some herbal tea.'

'No chance of that,' said Holly. 'The electricity has been turned off. We can't boil the kettle. You'll have to make do with some orange juice or something.'

Tracy sidled up to Holly. 'Who's the guy with the clipboard?' she whispered. Holly looked over her shoulder. Tony Blake was in the hall just outside the kitchen door, apparently busily engaged in writing notes.

Holly explained who he was.

'A surveyor?' said Belinda. 'That's a good sign, isn't it? If you've got surveyors in, doesn't it mean the work's almost done?'

'I *wish*,' sighed Holly.

She found Philip's phone number and dialled.

'There's bread in the bin,' she told Belinda. 'And some cheese in the fridge.'

'Great,' said Belinda. 'Cheese sandwiches. Got any pickle?'

Holly put the receiver to her ear. 'There's some funny noises going on down here,' she said, frowning at a series of whirrs and clicks on the line.

'Perhaps someone's drilled through the phone line?' said Tracy. 'I wouldn't be surprised. We had a guy in to fix the lights in our sitting-room once. After he'd gone we tried the switch and every light in the house went off. It was a week before we got things back to normal.'

'No,' said Holly. 'It's OK. I can hear it ringing.'

Mrs Owen picked up the phone. Holly asked to speak to Jamie. In the silence that followed Mrs Owen putting the receiver down, Holly heard a regular burring sound, as if she had a crossed line and someone else was trying to dial.

'There's definitely something wrong here,' said Holly. 'Come and listen.'

The three girls crowded around the receiver.

As they listened, the burring stopped with a loud click and they heard a tinny voice.

'That's an answering machine,' said Belinda. 'You must have a fault on your line.'

'I'd better put the phone down and dial again,' said Holly.

'That won't work,' said Belinda. 'If the phone

is off the hook at the other end you'll still be connected, whatever you do.'

'Shhh!' said Tracy. 'Listen!'

The answering machine message had ended and the clear voice of an excited-sounding woman could be heard.

'It's Tessa,' said the voice. 'I'm in Brompton. I think I've found out where there's a copy of the book with the Duke's poem in it. In the very village where it all took place. It looks like we're finally going to discover where the amulet was hidden. I'll phone you back at three o'clock to confirm. I shan't be able to get over there for a few days. Speak to you later, I hope. Bye.'

There was a brief hum and then the line seemed to clear.

'I wonder what that was all about?' said Tracy. 'She sounded very pleased with herself, whatever it was.'

'It's none of our business,' said Belinda. 'It's not very polite to eavesdrop on other people's conversations.'

'We were hardly eavesdropping,' said Holly. 'And it was hardly a conversation either.'

'What do you want?' came Jamie's voice down the phone. He sounded less than pleased at being disturbed.

'Mum says you're to come home and do your chores,' said Holly.

'I'm busy,' said Jamie. 'Tell her you couldn't find me. I'll do them all tomorrow.'

'I'm not telling her anything of the sort,' said Holly. 'You get over here, pest, or there'll be trouble.'

A loud groan sounded down the phone.

'Tell you what,' said Holly. 'Come over straight-away and I'll do you some lunch, how's that?'

Jamie grumbled something that Holly didn't quite catch and put the phone down.

Belinda gave Holly a beaming smile. 'Did some-one mention lunch?' she said. 'That's the best idea I've heard since breakfast.'

Holly grinned. 'OK,' she said. 'We might as well all have lunch – at least the gas is connected. But if Jamie's not back in half an hour I'm going to phone Mum and tell her.'

The three girls were just laying the table for lunch when Jamie came in, sniffing the air like a hound.

'What have you cooked me?' he asked.

'Sausage, egg, baked beans, mushrooms and tomatoes,' recited Belinda, filling four plates. She grinned. 'Just what we need to keep the cold out.'

Jamie slumped on to a chair. 'I'm exhausted,' he said. He grinned. 'Philip's got a mega-brilliant new computer game. I'm going to do my chores as quick as I can, then I'm going back over there. His mum said I can stay over for the night.'

'If your room's not tidy by the time Dad gets back you won't be going anywhere,' said Holly.

The four of them sat down to eat.

'You'd better tell Philip's mother there's something wrong with her phone when you go back,' said Tracy.

Jamie looked at her, his mouth full of sausage. 'Like what?' he mumbled.

'We heard a crossed line,' said Holly.

'What did you hear?' asked Jamie. 'Anything interesting?'

'Not especially,' began Holly, but Tracy interrupted her.

'A woman left a message on an answering machine,' she said.' 'Something about a book and a duke and an amulet.'

Jamie frowned. 'What's an amulet?'

'It's a sort of pendant that hangs from a necklace,' said Belinda. 'A kind of good-luck charm.'

'What did she say about it?' asked Jamie.

'Not much,' said Tracy. 'She said she'd phone the person back at three o'clock to explain.'

A grin expanded across Jamie's face. 'Are you going to listen in?'

'Certainly not,' said Holly. She frowned at Tracy. 'I wasn't going to mention any of this in front of *him*,' she said. 'You know how nosy he is.'

'I am not,' said Jamie. 'You three are the nosy ones round here. You just don't want me to know,

12

'cos you think there's some big mystery about it and you don't want to let me in on it. I bet you're going to listen in at three o'clock.'

'For the last time,' said Holly, 'we're *not* going to listen in.' She heard footsteps and turned to see Tony Blake come into the kitchen.

He smiled. 'Sorry to disturb you,' he said. 'Something smells good. I've just got to check a few things in here, if that's all right.'

'Of course,' said Holly. 'How's it going? Is everything looking OK?'

Tony Blake nodded. 'With any luck all the major work should be finished in a few weeks,' he said. 'I don't suppose you'll be sorry to hear that.'

'Hardly,' said Holly with a smile.

While they finished eating, Tony Blake wandered around the kitchen scribbling notes down on his clipboard.

The girls stacked the plates and Holly turned to Jamie.

'You can wash up,' she told him. 'And then you'd better get down to some work before Dad gets home.'

'Yes, sir,' said Jamie, giving her a mock salute. 'Any more orders, sir?'

Holly shook her head. 'You're such a comedian, Jamie.' She looked round at her friends. 'Coming?' she asked.

The three girls went back up to Holly's room to carry on planning their board game.

Some time later they heard the sound of the vacuum cleaner from Jamie's room.

'That's good,' said Holly. 'At least the electricity's back on. That means we can boil the kettle for a hot drink.'

She crossed the landing to Jamie's room.

'Jamie? Do you want a drink of . . .' Her voice trailed off. The vacuum cleaner was lying on the carpet in the middle of his room, roaring away. But there was no sign of Jamie. Puzzled, she switched it off.

Where was he? And why should he have left the cleaner on? A sudden suspicion dawned in Holly's mind. She glanced at the clock on Jamie's bedside table.

Three minutes past three. Three minutes after the time that the woman had said she would be phoning again on that crossed line.

Holly ran downstairs.

She nearly bumped into Tony Blake, who was standing just outside the kitchen door.

'Sorry,' she said. 'Excuse me.'

Jamie was sitting at the table, the telephone receiver to his ear, his hand over the mouthpiece as he scribbled something on a sheet of paper.

'Jamie!' shouted Holly.

He made frantic signs to her to keep quiet.

Ignoring him, she slammed her hand down on the button that cut the telephone line.

'Jamie!' yelled Holly. 'What do you think you're doing?'

'Hey!' Jamie glared at her. 'What did you do that for?'

'To stop you eavesdropping,' said Holly. 'I told you not to.'

'No, you didn't,' said Jamie. 'You just said *you* weren't going to. I've missed the end of what she was saying now, thanks to you!'

'Good!' said Holly. 'You shouldn't have been listening in the first place.'

'You won't say that when you find out what I've heard,' said Jamie. 'Look.' He waved the sheet of paper in front of her.

She looked at what he had written.

The Bad Luck Duke. Very valuable amulet. Gilchrist's Book-shop. Poetry book. Two days' time. Catching 3.15 train from Brompton. Should arrive 3.45.

Holly grabbed the sheet of paper from him and screwed it up in her fist.

'Don't do that!' yelled Jamie. 'Didn't you see? She said the Bad Luck Duke's amulet was incredibly valuable. We could look for it. We've got enough clues now.' He looked excitedly at her. 'There might be a reward for finding it,' he said. 'We could split the money. I'd be able to buy a new computer.' His eyes gleamed. 'I'd be able to buy a hundred new computers and all the games I could want!'

'No, we can't,' said Holly. 'You can't listen in on other people's conversations like that, Jamie. It's wrong.' She walked over to the rubbish bin, lifted the lid, and dropped the screwed up sheet of paper inside.

'I hate you, Holly Adams,' said Jamie. 'I know what you're up to. You want this mystery all to yourself!'

'No, I don't,' said Holly. 'It's nothing to do with us. Forget about it, Jamie. Now, you'd better get up there and finish your room, or I'll tell Dad what you've been up to, and you *will* be in trouble.'

With a final defiant glare, Jamie stamped upstairs.

As she left the kitchen, Holly saw that Tony Blake was still standing outside the door. He must have heard everything. He gave her a sympathetic smile.

'Kid brothers, eh?' he said.

'Tell me about it,' sighed Holly. 'Still, my dad should be home soon, so you'll be able to have a word with him.'

'That's good,' said Tony Blake. 'I've all but finished checking round.'

Holly went back up to the others. She told them about catching Jamie listening in on the crossed line.

16

'You've got to admit,' said Tracy, 'it is kind of intriguing, isn't it? A valuable amulet hidden away somewhere, and us with all these clues as to where it can be found.'

'I hope you're not suggesting we should try hunting for it,' said Belinda. 'I've been on enough wild goose chases for my liking. Besides it wouldn't be very fair.'

'Oh, I know,' agreed Tracy. 'But couldn't we just take a look at the information we've got? You know, just to see if we *could* figure it out if we wanted to? There's no harm in that, surely?'

'I suppose not,' said Holly. She knew she shouldn't, but the more they talked about it, the more intrigued she became. And after all, Jamie need never know. Holly smiled. 'It might be fun. I'll tell you what, I'll go and get Jamie's scribbles and we'll see what we can work out from what he overheard.'

On her way downstairs, Holly was surprised to see Tony Blake through the open front door, heading towards his van.

That's odd, she said to herself. *I thought he wanted to talk to my dad*. As she watched from the hallway, Tony Blake climbed into his van and drove rapidly away.

She shrugged, assuming that something important had come up that he had to deal with.

She went into the kitchen. She lifted the lid of the

17

bin. The scrunched-up piece of paper should have been at the top. But it wasn't there.

'Jamie!' cried Holly. 'The little monster!'

It seemed obvious to Holly what had happened. Jamie had sneaked down and taken the paper out of the bin.

She ran up to his room.

There was no sign of him. He had crept out of the house without finishing his chores. Despite everything she had said to him, it looked as if he intended searching for the amulet after all.

2 The mystery pest

'So where do you think he's gone?' asked Tracy
after Holly had told them about the disappearance
of both Jamie and the slip of paper.

'That's obvious, isn't it?' said Belinda. 'He's off
on a treasure hunt.'

'But I told him not to,' said Holly. She thumped
down on the bed. 'He never pays any attention to
me. And now I suppose I'll get told off by Mum for
not making sure he tidied his room. He should have
a health warning tattooed on his forehead. "Beware
– this boy can seriously irritate you."' She shook her
head. 'He won't *find* the amulet. He's probably not
even going to look for it properly. He's just doing
it to annoy me.'

'If I were you,' said Tracy, 'I'd think of some way
of getting even with him.'

'That's a thought,' said Belinda. 'What could you
do that would really drive him crazy?'

Holly thought for a moment. 'Strangle him?' she
suggested.

'That's a possibility,' Belinda said thoughtfully.
'Where would you hide the body, though?'

19

Tracy grinned. 'And your folks would probably miss him after a while,' she said.

'I doubt it,' said Holly. 'They'd probably give me a medal.' She sat upright, her hand to her chest. 'For services to humankind,' she announced, 'Holly Adams is hereby awarded the golden star for the well-deserved murder of Jamie Adams, known to the world as That Pest.'

'I know what would *really* get to him,' said Tracy. 'If we worked out all the clues ourselves. If we figured out where the amulet was hidden before he did.'

A gleam came into Holly's eyes. 'We could, couldn't we?' she said. 'I'd love that. He thinks he's so clever. It would annoy him no end if he got home and I could say, "Oh, by the way Jamie, the amulet is hidden at so-and-so place. Fancy you not being able to work it out."'

'*If* he doesn't work it out,' said Belinda.

'Of course he won't,' said Holly. 'He'll just run around like a headless chicken all afternoon.'

'Can you remember what he wrote down?' asked Tracy.

Holly nodded. 'Every word,' she said.

'Right,' said Belinda. 'Get the notebook, Holly. Let's get to work.'

Holly opened The Mystery Club's red notebook at a clean page. She sucked thoughtfully at the end of her pen for a moment, then wrote:

The Hidden Amulet, or The Downfall of Jamie Adams.

1. The Bad Luck Duke. Who is the Duke?

2. The book with the poem is in Gilchrist's bookshop. But where is that?

3. 'Tessa'. She said she was in Brompton and would be catching the 3.15 train, in two days' time, and arriving at her destination at 3.45. Where is she going?

'OK,' said Holly. 'What do we know so far? It seems to me that this duke person must know where the amulet is hidden.'

'Maybe he hid it,' said Tracy. 'And then put some kind of clue in this book Tessa was talking about. It's a pity she didn't say what he was the duke of. If we knew who he was, we'd be able to figure out where he came from. I mean, how many dukes can there be around here?'

'He may not even *be* from around here,' said Holly. 'Just because this Tessa woman was speaking from Brompton, it doesn't follow that the place where she thinks she'll be able to find the book is local. It could be anywhere.'

'Excuse me,' said Belinda. 'Aren't you missing something?'

Holly and Tracy looked round at her. Belinda was stretched out on the bed in her favourite 'thinking' pose.

'Like what, brainbox?' asked Tracy.

'Well,' said Belinda, 'Brompton is north-east of here – not all that far away. About thirty kilometres

21

at most.' She sat up. 'Have you got a map?' she asked Holly.

'Of course,' said Holly. She took down a map of Yorkshire from a shelf and opened it out on the carpet.

Belinda leaned over and pointed.

'There *we* are,' she said. 'And there's Brompton. That black line is the railway, right? Tessa said she was going to catch the 3.15 from Brompton, which would get her wherever she was going by 3.45. So all we've got to do is work out how far a train can get in half an hour, and we'll know where the bookshop is.'

Tracy ran her finger along the black railway line from Brompton. There were several stops close to one another in both directions. 'What speed do trains go at?' she said. 'How far could it go in thirty minutes, do you think?'

Belinda rolled on to her back, laughing.

Tracy frowned at her. 'What's so funny? How else are we going to work it out?'

'Ever heard of train timetables?' asked Belinda.

Holly jumped up. 'I think there's a book of train times downstairs,' she said. As she headed out of the room, she heard Tracy's voice:

'You know, Belinda, there are times when you're so sharp I'm surprised you don't cut yourself.'

Holly walked downstairs. There was something strange about the house. And then she realised. It was getting warmer. The front door was closed. She listened. There was no sound of workmen any more. Blessed silence! They must have finished for the day.

She found the train timetable book in the cupboard under the stairs. She picked up the local Yellow Pages as well and went back to her room.

It took a lot longer than they had expected to try and fathom the timetable. It was a thick book, its pages filled with tiny lists.

'I'm glad we're not planning a real journey,' said Tracy. 'We'd have missed about ten trains already, trying to figure out all this.'

'Got it!' said Belinda. She flattened the book out with her hands. 'This is the one. The train stops at Brompton at three fifteen and then, at three forty-five it stops again at a place called Lychthorpe. That's got to be it. Lychthorpe.'

'And look,' said Tracy, leaning over Belinda's shoulder. 'That train passes through Mosley. That's not far from here. There's a bus which goes there. So if we wanted, we could catch the bus to Mosley and pick up the train there.'

'Except that we don't actually want to go there,' Holly pointed out. While Belinda had been going through the timetables, she had been trying to find Gilchrist's bookshop in the Yellow Pages. Without any luck. Gilchrist's, it seemed, wasn't listed.

'I don't see why we shouldn't,' said Belinda.

23

'Imagine Jamie's face if we could tell him we'd actually been to the bookshop.'

'We might even be able to find the poetry book,' said Holly, fired by a new enthusiasm.

'I thought we weren't really going to look for the amulet,' said Tracy.

'We're not,' said Holly. 'But we could at least go there and have a look.'

Tracy glanced at her watch. 'Not today, we can't,' she said. 'I've got to go in a minute. My violin lesson starts in half an hour, and I'm not letting you two head off on any mysteries without me, that's for sure.'

Holly wrote 'Lychthorpe' in their notebook. At least now they had one bit of information that she was certain Jamie wouldn't have managed to work out.

'I'd better be going as well,' said Belinda, getting up and putting her coat on. 'And I've got to admit, I don't really fancy traipsing around the country in search of some amulet we don't really want to find, just to teach Jamie a lesson.'

'No, I suppose not,' said Holly. 'But at least we know we *could* do it if we wanted to.'

The thick dark clouds seemed so low that they almost scraped the rooftops as Holly let her two friends out.

Tracy shivered, pulling her coat round herself.

'You know they've forecast snow in the next couple of days?' she said.

'I hate snow,' Belinda complained. 'You know what it's like around here? Three flakes of snow fall and everything comes to a grinding halt.' She stamped off down the path. 'Snow should be banned!' she called back. 'There ought to be a law against it!'

'Don't be so miserable,' said Holly. 'Snow is lovely.'

'No, it isn't,' said Belinda. 'It looks pretty for about half an hour and then it just lies there for days getting muddy and slushy and revolting.' She grinned back. 'Anyway,' she said, 'those forecasts are always wrong. If they've said we'll have snow, there'll probably be a heat wave. Are you coming, Tracy?'

Holly waved goodbye then closed the door against the chill air.

She ran upstairs, looking forward to a few minutes of peace, during which she would be able to find out finally whether Juliana Moon was about to be confronted by the thing in the attic.

'Holly! I'm back!'

Holly closed her book on Chapter Seven. It was her father's voice. She ran downstairs. He was in the hall, unwrapping a scarf from round his neck.

'It's freezing out,' he said. 'How did everything go?'

'Fine, as far as I know,' said Holly. 'The workmen have gone already. I thought you'd be home ages ago.'

Mr Adams rolled his eyes. 'So did I,' he said. 'I couldn't get away. Daniel Parker got me involved in a long conversation about antiques.' He hung his coat up and Holly followed him into the kitchen. 'I couldn't really tell him to shut up after the order he'd given me.'

'What does he want you to do?' asked Holly.

Mr Adams grinned, rubbing his hands together. 'He wants six wheel-back chairs and a coffee table. And that's just for starters. If he likes them, he's got a list as long as your arm of other stuff he wants me to make.' He gave Holly a hug. 'I couldn't just rush off after an order like that, could I?'

In London, Mr Adams had been a successful solicitor, but his heart hadn't been in it for a long time. His secret ambition had always been to give up his job and concentrate on the work he really loved, making furniture. When Holly's mother had been offered the managership of the Willow Dale branch of the bank she worked for, it had been the perfect opportunity for Mr Adams to fulfill his dreams: to uproot himself from his old job and start again in an entirely new place.

26

He had a workshop in the garden, in which he produced beautiful items of furniture, and it hadn't taken long for him to start making a steady living from his craftsmanship. There seemed no end of people in and around Willow Dale who wanted to have a few Adams Workshop originals in their homes.

'The man from the surveyors came,' Holly told him as she switched the kettle on. 'He had a good look round, but then he went. You wanted to speak to him, didn't you?'

'Yes,' said Mr Adams. He looked at his watch. 'I'll give their office a ring now. He'll probably still be there. Did he say much? Did he seem satisfied with what we've had done?'

'I don't know,' said Holly. 'Shall I start dinner? Mum should be home soon.'

Mr Adams smiled. 'That's a good girl,' he said. 'Where's Jamie?'

'Don't ask,' sighed Holly.

'If he hasn't tidied his room, your mother is going to hang him out to dry,' said Mr Adams. 'He's been putting off doing it all week.'

It went through Holly's mind to tell her father about Jamie's escapades, but it wasn't in her nature to cold-bloodedly get anyone into trouble – not even Jamie.

'I think he'd just about finished doing it before he went out,' said Holly. 'Oh, by the way, there's some sort of fault on the phone line. I noticed it earlier.'

Mr Adams lifted the receiver and listened.

'It sounds OK now,' he said. He winked at Holly. 'Calling all cars,' he said into the mouthpiece. 'Be on the look-out for a small, mischievous whirlwind that answers to the name of Jamie Adams. Do not approach the suspect, he is armed and legged and highly dangerous.'

'You can say that again!' said Holly with a laugh.

Mr Adams dialled a number while Holly tipped a bag of potatoes into the sink and ran some water over them.

She was only half-listening to her father as she scrubbed the potatoes.

'Could I speak to Tony Blake, please?' said Mr Adams. 'Oh, isn't he? Have you any idea when he's expected?' There was a brief pause. 'Oh. OK. No, it's nothing vital. I'll phone tomorrow.' He put the phone down.

'No luck?' asked Holly.

'He hasn't been there this afternoon, apparently,' said Mr Adams. He smiled. 'It sounded as though they'd like to know where he is as well. I got the impression there's something going on over there.'

Holly carried on preparing the evening meal. Her father did a quick tour of the house to check

28

that the workmen had done everything they were supposed to have done.

Half an hour later, Mrs Adams arrived home from the bank.

The meal was almost ready, and there was still no sign of Jamie.

'It's his own fault if he misses dinner,' said Mrs Adams, as she laid the table. 'He knows what time we eat in this house.'

'I think he said something about staying over at Philip's tonight,' said Holly.

Mrs Adams laughed. 'I should think Mrs Owen will be sick of the sight of him by now,' she said. 'I don't know why he doesn't just move in over there. Still, I'll give her a ring a bit later, just to check he's not being a nuisance.'

'What, Jamie?' Holly said in mock surprise. 'A nuisance? Surely not?'

They were in the middle of their meal in the dining-room when the phone rang.

'I'll get it,' said Holly.

She picked up the phone in the hall.

'Jamie?' she said recognising her brother's voice. 'Just a second.' She closed the dining-room door and went back to the phone.

'Where have you been?' she whispered. 'What have you been up to?'

'Mind your own business,' said Jamie. 'I just

29

phoned to let Mum know Philip's mum says I can stay the night.'

'Never mind about that,' said Holly. 'I know you took that piece of paper out of the bin.'

'No, I didn't,' said Jamie. 'I never touched it.'

'Don't lie to me, Jamie,' said Holly. 'I went straight back down to the kitchen after I'd spoken to you, and it had gone. It didn't sprout legs and *walk* away on its own.'

'I don't know what you're talking about,' said Jamie. 'I didn't need that bit of paper anyway. I'm not so stupid that I couldn't remember what I'd written down.' A triumphant tone came into his voice. 'Philip and I have been working on the clues for finding that amulet, whether you like it or not, so there!'

'You and Philip?' said Holly. 'You two couldn't find a staircase in a lighthouse.'

'Want a bet?' crowed Jamie. 'For your information, big-head, we've already figured out where the bookshop is.'

'I don't believe you,' said Holly.

'We have!' said Jamie.

'So where is it?' asked Holly.

'Oh, sure!' said Jamie. 'I'm bound to tell *you*, aren't I? So you and your stupid Mystery Club friends can join in the hunt. Forget it, Holly. Philip and I are going to find this amulet. You three can go and whistle for it!'

'As it happens, beetle-brain, we already know where the bookshop is,' said Holly. 'It took us about ten seconds to work *that* one out.'

'Ha!' said Jamie. 'I knew it all along. You *are* looking for it. You just can't bear the thought of Philip and me getting there first. Well, hard luck, Holly, we're going over there tomorrow. *And* we're going to find the amulet, *and* we're going to get the reward. You might as well give up now.'

'Don't bet on it, Jamie,' said Holly, irritated by the mocking tone in her brother's voice. 'If it's a race you want, you can have one.'

'That suits me,' said Jamie. 'It's about time your dopey Mystery Club was put in its place. You three think you're so clever, don't you? Well, we'll see who's really the clever one in this family. And I'll tell you something right now – it isn't you!'

Holly jerked her head away as Jamie slammed the phone down.

'OK, little brother,' Holly said softly as she put the receiver back on to its cradle. 'If that's how you want it, that's the way you're going to get it. We'll soon show you who the real detectives are around here!'

3 Jamie gets there first

'Good heavens!' exclaimed Mr Adams as Holly appeared fully dressed at the kitchen door early the next morning. 'What are you doing up at this hour?'

'You make it sound like a miracle,' Holly said, affronted. 'I don't spend all day in bed, you know.'

Holly's parents were in the middle of breakfast. Mrs Adams looked round the side of her newspaper. 'You are on holiday, love,' she said. 'I'd make the most of it, if I were you.'

Holly walked over to the table, picking up a triangle of toast and borrowing her father's knife to spread some butter on it.

'I've got things to do,' she said. 'I can't afford to leave it too late.'

Mr Adams looked suspiciously at her. 'You're not off on one of your madcap investigations, are you?' he said.

'No,' said Holly. She smiled. 'Well, *sort* of, in a

32

way. But it's nothing like you're imagining, Dad. It's all perfectly safe.'

'Hmm,' came Mrs Adams' voice from behind the newspaper. 'I've heard that one before.'

'No, honestly,' said Holly. 'I've got a bet on with Jamie that I can get somewhere before he can, that's all it is.' She smiled. 'There's absolutely no chance of anything peculiar happening, I promise.'

Holly put her coat on and went round to the garage to get her bike. The grass on the front lawn was crisp and silvery with frost, but Holly was glad to feel that the biting north-easterly wind had died down.

All that was needed now was for a gentle southern breeze to come and blow the clouds away.

Her breath steamed out behind her as she set off. It didn't take her long to get to the street of terraced houses where Tracy and her mother lived.

'Hello,' said Mrs Foster, spotting Holly arriving on her bike as she was getting into her car. 'You're an early bird.'

Holly laughed. 'Everyone's saying that,' she said. 'Is Tracy up?'

'You know Tracy,' said Mrs Foster. 'She's been up for ages. She's been out for her run already.'

Mrs Foster let Holly in. Tracy was up in her bedroom, doing some post-running exercises on the floor, still in leggings and t-shirt.

'You're up early,' said Tracy, jumping up.

'What's wrong? Did your bed catch fire, or something?'

'If I hear any more comments about me being up early, I'm going to scream,' said Holly. 'Come on, get some proper clothes on. We've got things to do.'

'Like what?' asked Tracy.

While Tracy got herself into some warmer clothes, Holly told her about the conversation she'd had with Jamie on the phone the previous evening.

'Aha!' said Tracy. 'So we *are* going to look for the amulet. Great!'

'Only to shut Jamie up,' said Holly. 'I'm not having him going around bragging about how he beat us. I'll never hear the end of it.'

'Of course,' said Tracy, as they went downstairs, 'you do realise the biggest obstacle we've got to get over before we even start, don't you?'

'No,' said Holly. 'What?'

Tracy grinned. 'Getting Belinda out of bed,' she said.

'What?' Belinda sat up in bed, her hair a tangled mess, and groped for her spectacles. She jammed them on and looked at her bedside clock. 'Do you know what time it is?' she said. 'What are you? A pair of insomniac larks, or something?'

'It's not that early,' said Holly. 'We've got to get over to Lychthorpe before Jamie and Philip.'

The two of them peeled Belinda's duvet off and dragged her out of bed, while Holly did her best to explain to their grumbling friend the reason for their visit.

'They can have the blessed amulet, for all I care,' said Belinda, wistfully eyeing her warm bed as she pulled her jeans on. 'At least let's have some breakfast before we go.'

'No time,' said Holly.

'Yes, but—'

'No time for that either,' said Tracy.

Had Belinda been wider awake, she might have protested more vigorously. But as it was, she found herself in her coat and walking off to the bus stop with her two lively friends almost before she knew what was happening to her.

Tracy and Holly had cycled up the long hill to Belinda's huge house, but it was too far a journey to the railway station at Mosley for bikes in this weather. Especially when a warm bus would take them all the way there.

The country bus came rumbling up within minutes and the three girls got on board.

'I'm still half asleep,' complained Belinda, lolling her head on Holly's shoulder.

'I can soon cure that,' said Tracy, opening a window so that a draught of cold air came blowing in over Belinda's face. 'Better?' she asked. 'Are you waking up now?'

Belinda eyed her gloomily. 'Yes,' she said. 'Thanks. You're a real pal.'

The bus stopped in the carpark behind the railway station in Mosley.

'Quick!' shouted Holly. 'There's a train!'

The three girls ran for the train.

'What about tickets?' puffed Belinda.

'We'll get them at the other end,' said Holly, as they jumped into a carriage.

'I don't care what either of you says,' declared Belinda as she slumped into a seat. 'The moment we get to Lychthorpe, I'm looking for something to eat.'

'If you got up at a reasonable hour,' said Tracy, 'you'd have had time for breakfast. Stop moaning.' She looked at Holly. 'You don't think Jamie will have got there before us, do you?'

'I hope not,' said Holly. She shook her head. 'I doubt it,' she added. 'He's no better at getting out of bed than Belinda.'

There were two stops before the train pulled into the small, ramshackle station at Lychthorpe. No one else got off, and the platform was deserted.

They went to the ticket window and paid for their journey, then came out into what seemed to be open countryside. Tall, bare trees hemmed the station. Through the spider's web of branches they could see a stone tower. It was square and solid, with a flat roof and a clockface set high in its wall.

A small, thin man in a blue railway uniform was sweeping the tarmac.

Holly approached the man. 'Excuse me,' she said. 'We're looking for a bookshop called Gilchrist's. Could you give us directions?'

'Gilchrist's?' said the man, leaning on his broom. 'It's over in the village. You'll have to go over the level-crossing. Follow the road until you get to the green. Cross the green and it's in the street almost directly opposite. Sawyer Street. You can't miss it.'

'What's that building over there?' asked Tracy, pointing to the tower.

'That's St Jerome's church,' said the man. 'You don't want to go that way. The village is over yonder.' He nodded his head to the other side of the railway lines.

'Thanks,' said Holly. 'Sawyer Street, you say?'

'That's right,' said the man, resuming his slow sweeping.

The girls headed for the level-crossing. It was a modern, automatic half-barrier type, with a gated footpath to one side.

They checked both ways along the steel railway lines, then crossed over towards the village.

It was much smaller than Willow Dale: a pretty collection of old houses that seemed to huddle together against the cold. A real old-fashioned Yorkshire village of quiet, narrow streets.

The village green was a square of grass and bushes, circled by black railings. Tracy spotted a gateway and they followed her in and along the path that took them to the far side.

'Look,' breathed Holly. 'A robin!' They paused to watch the small red-breasted bird as it hopped to and fro under the eaves of a naked bush.

'Poor little thing,' said Tracy. 'It must be half starved at this time of year.'

'I know how it feels,' said Belinda. 'Can we look for a shop that sells food before we do anything else?'

'No,' said Holly unfeelingly. 'Gilchrist's first, food later.'

They came out of the green and crossed the road, their eyes peeled for Sawyer Street amongst the side roads that led from the square.

'Here we are,' said Holly, seeing a sign. She grinned round at her friends. 'I can't wait to see Jamie's face when we tell him we got here first.'

There were a few people on the street, and the occasional car. Gilchrist's was a narrow shop with dingy bottle-glass windows and peeling brown paint.

A dull bell chimed as they pushed the door open. The musty smell of old paper greeted them. It was more like an abandoned storeroom than a shop. A maze of dark, wood display shelves created narrow aisles, piled with books which the girls had to step gingerly over as they made their way through.

'Phew,' breathed Tracy. 'It's like something out of a Charles Dickens novel. Just you wait, any second now Oliver Twist is going to pop his head up and ask us what we want.'

Holly looked around. None of the shelves seemed to be labelled. As far as she could tell, the books were heaped on the shelves at random.

'We'll never find anything by ourselves,' she said. 'I wonder where the shopkeeper is?'

'If he's anything like the shop,' said Belinda, 'we'll probably find him lying dead somewhere in a heap of dust.'

All three of them jumped with surprise as the grey-haired head of an elderly man appeared suddenly from behind some shelves.

'I'm not quite dead yet, my dear,' he said, straightening up, his arms full of books. 'Can I help you?'

Belinda blushed scarlet. 'Sorry,' she said. 'I didn't see you there.'

'No matter,' said the man with a toothy grin. 'I've heard worse.' He circled the shelf. He was tall and terribly thin, wearing a moth-eaten sweater and baggy brown corduroy trousers. 'Are you just browsing, or are you looking for something in particular?'

'We're looking for a poetry book,' said Holly, as a red faced Belinda sidled behind her, embarassed.

'Written by a duke,' added Tracy. 'Someone known as The Bad Luck Duke. It'll be something to do with a lost amulet.'

The man gave them a crocodile grin. 'Well, I never,' he said. 'So they weren't pulling my leg after all.'

'I beg your pardon?' said Holly.

The shopkeeper put his load of books down and headed towards the back of the shop.

The three girls looked at one another in confusion.

'Come,' said the man, beckoning to them. He stepped behind a low counter. 'Which of you three young ladies would be Holly Adams?'

'That's me,' said Holly, as they stepped up to the counter. 'But how . . .?'

The man opened a drawer and drew out a folded sheet of paper. 'I was asked to give this to you if you came in here.'

Holly stared at the piece of paper. 'I don't understand,' she said. 'What is it?'

'A young gentleman by the name of Jamie gave it to me,' said the shopkeeper. 'He was in here about half an hour ago with another young gentleman.'

'Jamie!' gasped Holly.

'He beat us to it!' said Tracy. 'The little beast beat us to it!'

Holly took the sheet of paper from the shop-keeper and unfolded it. Belinda and Tracy leaned over her shoulders. It was written in Jamie's spidery handwriting.

The Mystery Club is rubbish! they read. *We got here first*!

'As I told him,' said the shopkeeper, 'you're very lucky to find me open. I'm only planning on opening up for a couple of days this week: today and tomorrow. I have to drive all the way from Sheffield, you see. I took the shop over a few weeks ago. I'm really only sorting through the stock to see if there's anything of value before I sell the place. And you came all the way from Willow Dale especially to visit the shop, so the young gentleman said.'

'Did he get the book?' asked Belinda. 'Please, don't tell us you sold him the book.'

The grinning shopkeeper shook his head. 'He didn't get the book,' he said.

'Great!' said Tracy. 'So you've still got it? What happened, didn't he have enough money?'

'It was nothing to do with money,' said the shopkeeper. 'As I told them, I can't locate a book for you without a bit more to go on than it being a poetry book. There are hundreds of poetry books in stock. If I'm to find a particular volume, I'll need the name of the writer, or at least of the publisher.'

'It was written by a duke,' said Tracy. 'Isn't that

enough to go on? How many dukes write poetry, for heaven's sake?'

'I know of no poetry anthology written by a duke,' said the shopkeeper. 'I'll need his real name.'

'The Bad Luck Duke?' said Holly. 'Does that mean anything to you?'

'I'm afraid not,' said the man. 'I can only suggest to you what I suggested to the young gentlemen: go and find out some more about this book.'

'But we *know* it's here,' said Belinda. 'You've got it somewhere. Could we have a bit of a search round?'

'I don't think that's a very good idea,' said the man. 'No, you go and get me a name and I'll do what I can for you. Don't worry, I'm open all day today and tomorrow. You come back with a bit more information and I promise that if the book is here, I'll locate it for you.'

'And you told Jamie the same?' asked Holly.

'Exactly the same,' said the man, grinning again. 'What is this? Is it a competition? Something to do with school?'

'Something like that,' said Tracy. 'If the two boys come back before us with any more information, I don't suppose you could, kind of, pretend you can't find the book, could you?'

The shopkeeper frowned. 'That hardly sounds

42

fair,' he said. 'Especially if you're competing to find this book.'

'No, of course not,' said Holly, frowning at Tracy. She smiled at the shopkeeper. 'Thanks, anyway,' she said. 'And don't worry, *we'll* be back here first.'

The three girls left the shop.

'Fancy asking him to cheat for us,' Belinda said to Tracy.

Tracy shrugged. 'It was worth a try,' she said. 'We want to win, don't we? Have you got any better ideas?'

'I've got *one* better idea,' said Belinda. 'I'm going to find a shop that sells food. You two can do what you like.'

'We'll wait for you in the green,' said Holly. 'There's a bench there. We can have a sit down and decide what to do next.'

'Right,' said Belinda. 'I'll see you in a couple of minutes.'

She followed the pavement around, past a row of attractive terraced cottages with lacework curtains in the windows. She had looked for a confectioner's shop in Sawyer Street without luck. But she remembered noticing a row of shops over on the other side of the green.

Anything will do, she thought. *A bar of chocolate or a packet of crisps. Someone must sell something edible around here.*

She crossed the road. There was a bank, and a dress shop, and a brightly coloured shop that sold baby clothes. And then, on the corner, she spotted a bakery.

She grinned. *That'll do*, she thought, her mouth already watering at the idea of warm bread rolls. 'And to show what a good-natured person I am,' she said to herself, 'I'll even buy something for the others, despite them dragging me over here without any breakfast.'

She glanced down the sidestreet. A white van was parked with two wheels up on the pavement. She didn't pay it much attention, except to notice that the windows were steamed up. The thing that really drew her attention was a little way further along the road.

A boarded-up old pub. From a black iron frame hung a large square sign. It depicted the head and shoulders of a man. He wore a black cloak and an old fashioned black three-cornered hat. But it was the writing under the portrait that had caught her eye.

'*The Duke Oliver*.'

She walked along the street. The man on the sign wore a mask across his eyes, and in his two raised hands he held a brace of antique pistols.

'The Duke Oliver,' Belinda murmured to herself. 'The *Duke* Oliver.' Was it just a coincidence that the old pub should have the word 'duke' in its name?

Coincidence or not, she decided, it was definitely something that Holly and Tracy would be interested in hearing about.

Temporarily forgetting her hunger, Belinda ran back towards the green.

'So how are we going to find out any more about this book?' asked Tracy. She and Holly were sitting on the bench in the green.

'That's what I'm thinking about,' said Holly. 'How *do* you go about it? We don't have his name, or any idea what the book is called. We don't even know if this duke person wrote the entire book, or if it's a collection with just a couple of his poems in it.' She sighed. 'I've got a feeling we're wasting our time.'

'Look on the bright side,' said Tracy. 'If *we* can't get any further, then it's pretty unlikely that Jamie will either.'

'He managed to work out where the bookshop was,' said Holly. 'I'm beginning to think I've underestimated him, the pest. And if we *don't* get any further, then he's won, hasn't he? He got to the shop first. Jamie and Philip have beaten us.'

'Oh, come on,' said Tracy. 'We're not beaten yet. There must be some way of finding out who this duke guy is. Aren't there books that tell you all about the aristocracy?'

Holly stared at her. 'Have you any idea of how

45

many dukes there have been in this country?' she said. 'We don't even know when this Bad Luck Duke was alive. Even if there was a book like you mentioned, it'd take us weeks to go through it on the off-chance of finding some reference to him.'

'Ahem!' said a voice behind them. They looked round. It was Belinda. 'I think you might find his first name was Oliver,' she said.

Holly's eyes widened. 'Have you found out something?' she asked.

'Maybe,' said Belinda. 'It's a long shot, mind you.' She told them about the pub sign. 'Come and see for yourselves,' she said. 'See what you think.'

As they headed for the gateway out of the green, they heard the ferocious barking of a dog.

'What on earth?' The three girls stood on the pavement outside the gate. Racing towards them across the road were Jamie and Philip. Close on their heels was a large black alsatian, speeding after them and barking wildly.

'Help!' yelled Jamie, catching sight of Holly and her friends.

'Quick!' called Holly. 'In here.' She didn't have time to wonder what was going on. All she knew was that Jamie and Philip needed to be got out of harm's way.

The two boys made a run for the gate. Holly and her friends dived in after them and Holly just managed to snatch the gate closed in the fierce dog's face.

It jumped at the gate, claws scrabbling as its jaws snapped at Holly's hand.

'Hey!' A man's voice cut the air angrily. 'Hey! Stop! Stop those boys!'

Backing away from the gate, Holly saw a man come running across the road. A round-faced man with balding hair and red-framed glasses.

'It's Tony Blake!' she gasped, recognising the surveyor immediately.

But what was he doing there? And what had Jamie and Philip done that had made him so angry?

4 The Duke Oliver

'Stop those boys!' shouted Tony Blake, the tails of his coat flapping about his legs as he ran across the road towards Holly and the others.

'Mr Blake!' yelled Holly above the barking of the alsatian. 'It's us! It's me! Holly Adams!'

Tony Blake came to a panting halt, staring at Holly in amazement.

'Those boys,' he gasped, pointing over the railings at Jamie and Philip. 'They were interfering with my van.' He stared at Jamie, the anger fading from his face as he finally seemed to recognise Holly's brother.

'We weren't!' shouted Jamie. 'We weren't doing anything.'

'Could you get that dog under control?' said Belinda. 'You shouldn't allow dangerous animals like that to run around without a lead.'

Tony Blake slid his hand under the alsatian's collar. 'Luther! Down boy. Quiet now. Good boy,' he said. The dog stopped barking, its long tongue lolling out of the side of its mouth as it lifted its head to look at its master.

'Did you set that dog on my brother?' Holly said angrily.

'Of course not,' said Tony Blake.

'He did!' shouted Jamie. 'He told it to get us.'

Tony Blake looked flustered. 'How was I to know who it was?' he said. 'I thought they were a couple of young thieves.' He leaned to give the dog a hefty pat on the flank. 'Luther wouldn't have harmed them. I just wanted to scare them off.' A weak smile spread across Tony Blake's face. 'You can't blame me for protecting my property.' He looked at Holly. 'Your brother and his friend took me by surprise.' His eyes moved on to the two boys. 'You shouldn't go creeping around vans, you know,' he said. 'People could get the wrong idea.'

'We were only looking,' said Jamie.

'Of course you were,' said Tony Blake, an unconvincing air of friendliness edging into his voice. 'I can see that, now I know who you are.' He drew a lead out of his coat pocket and attached it to the dog's collar. 'Still,' he said, 'there's no harm done.' He gave a nod towards them. 'Well,' he said. 'I'd better be pressing on.'

Holly and the others watched as he pulled the dog away from the railings and walked quickly out of sight along the pavement.

'He looked a bit of a mess,' said Tracy. 'Did

you notice that coat? He looked like he'd been sleeping in it.'

'He was!' said Jamie. 'Wasn't he, Philip?'

Philip nodded. 'He was fast asleep in the van,' he said. 'If you ask me, he'd been there all night.'

'But what were you *doing*?' asked Holly.

Jamie grinned. 'Did you get our message in the shop?' he asked.

'Yes,' said Holly. 'We got the message. Stop trying to change the subject. I want to know why he set that dog on you.'

'I recognised his van,' explained Jamie. 'It's in a side street over there.' He pointed in the direction of the street where Belinda had seen the pub sign. 'We went to investigate. I didn't think he'd be in it.'

'Investigate?' said Tracy. 'Investigate what?'

Jamie gave her a patronising look. 'I don't see why we should tell you everything,' he said. 'Work it out for yourselves.'

Holly lunged forward, catching a handful of Jamie's collar. 'See those railings?' she said. 'If you don't tell us what you were up to, I'm going to jam your head through them, and you can stay there until the fire brigade comes along to rescue you. Got it?'

Jamie gave her a worried look. 'You're getting very aggressive, Holly,' he gasped. 'Is it because you're losing the race for the amulet? OK. Let me go, and I'll tell you.'

Holly released him.

'It's to do with that bit of paper,' explained Jamie. 'The one on which I wrote the stuff about the amulet.'

'What about it?' asked Holly.

'Well, you didn't take it out of the bin, did you?' said Jamie. 'And I know I didn't. But *someone* did, if it wasn't there any more. And the only other person who knew it was in there was that Blake man.'

'Why should he take it?' asked Holly. 'What makes you think he'd be in the least bit interested?'

'Because he heard me say that the amulet was worth a lot of money,' said Jamie. 'He was hanging about outside the kitchen while we were talking about it.'

'Rubbish,' said Holly.

'If it's rubbish, then why is he here?' demanded Jamie. 'He must have worked out where the bookshop was, just as Philip and I had. That's why we were looking in the van. To see if the bit of paper was there. We didn't realise he'd be sleeping in there.'

Holly laughed. 'And I'm supposed to be the one with the wild imagination,' she said. She shook her head. 'You're cracking up, Jamie. Never,' she added, 'never in a million years would someone like Tony Blake go to all that trouble because of some of your scribblings. Don't you think he's got better things to do with his time than go on some wild goose chase?'

'I don't know,' began Tracy, 'it is kind of—'

Holly glared her into silence. 'I think you and Philip ought to go home,' said Holly. 'Or would you rather I gave Dad a ring and told him what you've been up to?'

'You just want to try and stop us looking for the amulet,' exclaimed Jamie. 'That's cheating.'

'Forget about the amulet,' said Holly. 'There was never any chance of you finding it, anyway.'

'That's what you think,' said Jamie. 'Philip's got a book at home. A book all about the dukes and earls and barons that used to live around Yorkshire in the old days. We're going to find out about the Bad Luck Duke from that. And once we find out who he was, we're going to come back here and get his book.' He looked at Philip. 'Come on,' he said. 'Let's leave these *girls* to try and come up with their own ideas.'

Jamie opened the gate and the two boys set off towards the railway station.

'And don't you worry,' Jamie shouted back. 'When we find the amulet and get a write-up in the newspapers, I shan't forget to mention how useless the Mystery Club is!'

Holly said nothing as the two boys walked out of sight.

'It is a bit weird about the Blake guy being here, don't you think?' said Tracy.

'More than weird,' said Holly. 'I think Jamie might be right about him.'

Tracy stared at her. 'I was going to say that when you shut me up,' she said.

'I shut you up because I didn't want to talk about it in front of them,' said Holly. 'But Tony Blake *was* just outside the kitchen door when we were talking about the amulet. He could easily have seen me throw the paper in the bin. And that would explain why he left so quickly, when he was supposed to be staying to talk to my dad.'

'Hold everything,' said Belinda. 'If Tony Blake believes all this about the amulet and if he's interested enough to have worked out that the bookshop with the poetry book is here, how come he didn't get it yesterday?'

'He would have done if he could,' said Holly. 'Don't you get it? The shopkeeper said he's only opening up for two days. Today and tomorrow. So if Tony Blake got here yesterday, he'd have found the bookshop closed.'

'And he slept in his van overnight?' Tracy said disbelievingly. 'Why would he do *that*? Why didn't he just go home?'

'I don't know,' said Holly. 'But I can tell you one thing: he was definitely wearing the same clothes as yesterday. And when my dad phoned his office yesterday afternoon, they said he hadn't been back.'

'It's all a bit far-fetched,' said Tracy. 'Unless he's got some reason for not going home.'

'I'll tell you one thing that *is* suspicious,' said Belinda. 'Why didn't he comment on us all being here? If he just happened to be here by coincidence, you'd think he'd have been a lot more surprised to see us. But he didn't strike me as looking surprised. More sort of alarmed, if you ask me. And he disappeared quickly enough, didn't he?'

'Exactly,' said Holly. 'And I'd like to know what he's up to. Where did Jamie say his van was parked?'

'That way,' said Tracy, pointing. 'But if we're going to take a look, we'd better keep ourselves well out of sight. I don't fancy tangling with that dog.'

'Just a minute,' said Belinda. 'His van? It's white, isn't it?'

'That's right,' said Holly.

'I saw it,' said Belinda. 'Just now. It was parked in the same street as the pub.'

The three girls crossed the street away from the green, keeping themselves out of sight of the sidestreet. The occasional passer-by gave them looks of mild curiosity.

'Well?' asked Belinda, as they stood at the street

54

corner and Holly leaned round the wall to look down the sidestreet. 'See it?'

'No,' said Holly. She stepped out into the open. 'It's not there.'

Belinda followed her out. She pointed to the pavement opposite the pub. 'It was there,' she said. 'He must have decided to make himself scarce after seeing us.' She walked down the street. 'Come on,' she said. 'Come and look at this sign.'

They stood under the hanging painting of the masked man.

'He doesn't look much like a duke,' said Tracy. 'He's more like a highwayman.'

'But the pub's called The Duke Oliver,' said Belinda. 'There's got to be a link somewhere. Perhaps we should ask? Someone is bound to know. Let's try in here.' She headed into the shop next door to the boarded-up pub.

It was one of those small shops that sells everything from newspapers to groceries.

Belinda picked up a packet of biscuits and went to the counter, Tracy and Holly following in her wake.

'Do you know anything about that pub next door?' asked Belinda as she paid for the biscuits.

'All I know is that it's been empty for some years,' said the assistant. 'I'm not from around here, so I can't tell you much else. But if it's local history you're wanting to find out about, your best bet is to have a chat with the vicar. He knows all about this place, so they say.'

'Where would we find him?' asked Holly.

'He might be at the church, I suppose,' said the assistant. 'Over on the other side of the railway. If anyone can tell you about the pub, it'll be him.'

It wasn't a very large church. Built of grey stone, the most impressive part of it was the tall square tower with the ornate clock set in it. It lay behind a screen of trees, about fifty metres beyond the railway.

It was hemmed by a low stone wall, over which the girls could see a small graveyard. The gravestones were old and unkempt, some lying in the grass or leaning against the church walls, while others thrust up out of the ground at strange angles.

'It doesn't look like anyone's been buried here for ages,' said Belinda as they passed in through the gate at the front of the church. 'Can you read any of the inscriptions?'

Holly looked at a lichened and worn stone. The writing was only just visible.

'"Naomi Hawthorne",' she read. '"Beloved wife and mother, 1762 to 1794".' She looked around at her friends. 'Poor woman,' she said. 'She was only thirty-two when she died.'

'Life was brief and hard in those days,' said a strange voice. The girls looked round. A man in a flat cap and an anorak had come round the side of the church behind them. He was carrying a sack, out of which protruded the broken ends of twigs.

'Are you interested in graveyards?' he asked. 'Lots of people are.' He smiled bleakly. 'We get more people here looking at the old stones than we do to join the congregation these days,' he said.

'We were looking for the vicar, actually,' said Holly.

The man smiled. 'You've found him,' he said. 'I'm Colin Davies. I'm the vicar here. Did you want a look round the church? I keep it locked most of the time, but I can open up if you'd like to see inside.'

'I'm sure it's lovely,' said Belinda. 'But we really came here to ask about something else. We were told you were an authority on the village.'

The vicar smiled. 'Were you now? That's very kind of whoever told you. I don't know about being an *authority* exactly, but I do know a bit about the local area.'

'Do you know anything about The Duke Oliver?' asked Tracy.

'Oh, the pub?' said the vicar. 'There's certainly plenty to tell about that place.'

'Do you know who Duke Oliver was?' asked Holly. 'Was he anything to do with the Bad Luck Duke?'

'Duke Oliver *was* the Bad Luck Duke,' said the vicar.

'I knew it!' said Belinda. 'And what was he the duke of?'

The vicar laughed. 'He wasn't the duke of anything,' he said. 'That was his name. Oliver Duke. He was the landlord of the pub in the eighteenth century. But what no one realised at the time was that he was moonlighting.' The vicar's eyes sparkled with amusement. 'He was a highwayman,' he said. 'The pub was called The Three Feathers at the time. They only changed the name to The Duke Oliver after he'd been hanged.'

'A highwayman?' said Holly. 'No, that can't be right. He can't be the duke we're looking for. The one we want wrote poetry.'

'That's him,' said the vicar. 'He was apparently a very cultured man – very well-educated for the time. A real dandy highwayman, according to the stories,' he grinned. 'I can even show you where he is buried, if you're interested.'

He led the three girls round to the back of the church.

'In those days, people who had been executed couldn't be buried in consecrated ground,' he told them. 'So they were put to rest outside the confines of the churchyard.' He looked round at the girls. 'It seems a bit harsh,' he said. 'But things *were* harsh in those days.' The wall round the graveyard was punctuated at the back by a small gateway which led to a strip of rough ground bordered by an arc of woodland.

The vicar pointed to a gnarled old oak tree. 'Oliver Duke is buried under there,' he said. 'In an unmarked grave. It's all in the church annals, if anyone is interested enough to look.'

'Do you know anything about a hidden amulet?' asked Holly.

The vicar pursed his lips. 'The famous lost amulet, eh?' he said. He grinned. 'I know some of the folklore that's grown up around the amulet. Apparently, Oliver Duke waylaid a Spanish princess who was travelling through Yorkshire on her way to marry into the Scottish nobility. The amulet was part of the marriage dowry. It's supposed to be enormously valuable. It was never seen again. Some people believe it's still hidden around here somewhere, but my guess is his daughter took it away with her when she left the village.'

'He had a daughter?' said Holly.

'That's right,' said the vicar. 'Elizabeth. His only surviving child. She left Lychthorpe after her father was hanged. If you ask me, he passed the amulet on to her before they caught him.' He smiled. 'But that's not as much fun as believing it's still hidden around here somewhere, is it?'

'Nowhere *near* as much fun,' breathed Tracy.

'And there's more about Oliver Duke, if you're interested,' said the vicar, smiling round at the girls, enjoying their obvious interest. 'The authorities went to The Three Feathers to arrest Oliver Duke. They were certain he was in there, but when they searched there was no sign of him. He'd just vanished.'

'Vanished?' breathed Tracy. 'You mean, like, into thin air?'

'Apparently so,' said the vicar. 'But he didn't get far. They scoured the town for him and eventually brought him to bay over there.' He pointed to the oak tree. 'Where he gave himself up. He didn't really have much choice. They'd have killed him on the spot if he'd resisted. But he asked to be buried there. Under the oak tree.' The vicar smiled wanly. 'They took him to York assizes and three weeks later he was tried and hanged. His body was brought back here, and the vicar at the time allowed him to be buried where he'd asked. And as far as I know, that's the end of the story of the Bad Luck Duke.'

'But why was he called the Bad Luck Duke?' asked Belinda.

The vicar laughed. 'I'd have thought getting yourself hanged was reason enough, wouldn't you?' he said.

'Thanks for telling us about him,' said Holly.

'No trouble,' said the vicar. 'It's not often I get the chance to show off a bit.'

The three friends headed back towards the rail-way, chatting about their new discoveries.

'Do you think he's right about the daughter?' asked Tracy. 'Do you think Oliver Duke just gave the amulet to her?'

'I don't think so,' said Belinda. 'I think he left the poem for her as a clue. And why should he do that if he'd given the amulet to her?' Behind them they heard the clock in the church tower strike the hour.

'That's funny,' said Belinda, looking at her watch. 'It's midday, but the clock struck eleven.'

'You miscounted, I expect,' said Tracy. 'Look, you guys, I've got to get home. I promised my mom I'd help her in the nursery this afternoon.' She gave them a hopeful grin. 'I don't suppose you'd like to come with me, would you?'

'Why not?' said Holly. 'We can talk over what we've found out.'

They caught the train back to Mosley, and Belinda was finally able to satisfy her hunger by working her way right through the packet of biscuits.

'Any chance of lunch when we get there?' she asked, gazing into the empty packet.

Tracy laughed. 'I expect so,' she said.

'And then we'll write up our findings in the notebook,' said Holly. She grinned. 'So much for super-sleuth Jamie. He and Philip are going to be

61

wasting the rest of the day looking for a real duke in that book they were talking about. And we already know all about the Bad Luck Duke.' She stretched herself out on the train seat. 'The Mystery Club wins again!' she said.

Holly was hoping that Jamie would be around when she got home that evening. She was looking forward to asking him what he'd found out about Oliver Duke – especially as she knew he couldn't have found *anything* out at all.

She put the Mystery Club's notebook on her bedside table and went to his room. He was just coming out with his rucksack over his shoulder.

'Found anything interesting?' she asked.

'Not yet,' said Jamie. 'But we will. I'm spending the night at Philip's again. We're halfway through his book already, and we'll finish it tonight. So we'll have found out all about the duke by tomorrow, don't worry.'

Holly laughed. 'I'm not worried, Jamie,' she said. 'I'm not worried, because I know you're not going to find anything.'

'Take a bet on that?' said Jamie.

Holly shook her head. 'There's no point in *betting* with you,' she said. 'We already know all about him. And I'll give you one little clue, Jamie: you're not going to find him in that book of Philip's even if you search for the rest of your life!'

'You're bluffing,' said Jamie. 'You don't know anything.'

Holly smiled. 'If you say so,' she said making her way downstairs.

'You don't!' Jamie shouted after her. 'You're just pretending.'

Holly went into the sitting-room. A few minutes later she heard Jamie come stomping downstairs. He stuck his head round the door.

'See you tomorrow,' he said.

Mrs Adams looked round from the television. 'Behave yourself at Philip's,' she said. 'And don't eat them out of house and home.'

Jamie gave Holly a big grin. 'Finders keepers,' he said to her. 'And losers weepers.' He shut the door and they heard the front door close behind him.

'What was all that about?' asked Mr Adams.

'Nothing,' said Holly. 'Just a little race we've got going between us. A race that Jamie is going to lose.'

Later that evening Holly was sitting up in bed. Before she went to sleep she decided to have a last look at the notes she'd made about Oliver Duke.

She flipped through the red notebook.

'What on earth?' She stared at the book. The pages that contained all their findings about the Bad Luck Duke were missing. They'd been torn out.

'Jamie!' Holly gave an angry hiss. 'That little cheat!'

It was too late to do anything about it now, but first thing in the morning she was determined to go over to Philip's house and sort her little brother out once and for all.

She'd teach him a lesson he'd never forget!

5 The search for Jamie

Holly's anger at Jamie had not lessened overnight. If anything, it had increased. Where did that little devil get off? she thought. Tearing pages out of their notebook like that. When she caught up with him, she thought grimly, he'd wish he had never been born.

She went downstairs next morning, slightly irritated that she had overslept. Plotting revenges on Jamie had kept her awake half the night, and being tired only fuelled her anger.

Mrs Adams had gone to work, but Holly could hear her father talking on the telephone in the kitchen as she went down to the hall and put her coat on.

'What do you mean?' she heard her father say. 'He's still not in the office? He must have come back by now. This is ridiculous.'

Holly didn't pay attention – she had much more important things on her mind. She wound a scarf round her neck and went to the kitchen door.

Mr Adams was standing there with the receiver to his ear.

Holly tried to get his attention.

'Have you tried him at home?' she heard him ask. There was a pause. 'Oh, I see. Well, if you can't contact him, then I'll have to wait, won't I?' he said. 'But tell him to phone me the moment he appears, OK?' He put the phone down.

'Hello, Holly,' he said. 'Off out?'

'Yes,' said Holly. 'I'm going to Philip's house to find Jamie and murder him.'

Mr Adams nodded. 'Fair enough,' he said. 'Try not to get blood all over their carpet, though. I don't want to be sent a cleaning bill.' He smiled. 'Has Jamie annoyed you in some way?'

'You could say that,' said Holly. 'I'll see you later.'

It didn't seem as cold to Holly as it had been for the past few days. Not that it was warm, exactly, but the freezing wind had died down, leaving a dense layer of deep grey cloud over the town.

As Holly cycled to Philip's house, she tried to remember the last time she had seen a bit of blue sky. It seemed like ages ago. And there was a strange, sharp smell in the air. The smell of impending snow.

She rested her bike by the front gate and went up to the house.

Mrs Owen answered the bell.

'Hello, Holly,' she said. 'You're brave, coming out on your bike in this weather. Haven't you heard the forecast?'

'I'm afraid not,' said Holly. 'What forecast?'

'Snow,' said Mrs Owen. 'And lots of it. That's why I haven't let Philip out this morning. He catches cold very easily.'

'Is Jamie up yet?' asked Holly. 'Could I see him?'

'He's gone,' said Mrs Owen. 'He left about half an hour ago. I told him he should go straight home. He was planning some jaunt with Philip, but I said he'd be better off indoors. Didn't he go home, then?'

'I don't think so,' said Holly. 'I'd have seen him.'

Mrs Owen rolled her eyes. 'Boys!' she said. 'They're always up to some mischief, aren't they?'

'You can say that again,' Holly said feelingly. 'Thanks anyway. I think I probably know where to find him.'

Holly went back to her bike.

'OK, Jamie,' she said to herself. 'I know where you've gone, you little pest.' That much was obvious to Holly. Armed with the information he had stolen from The Mystery Club's notebook, Jamie had taken himself off back to the bookshop in Lychthorpe.

Fired by her anger, Holly cycled towards Tracy's house.

One way or another, before the day was out, she

was going to *get* that little brother of hers – and get him good!

'It's going to snow,' Belinda complained. 'It's going to snow two metres deep and we're all going to get pneumonia. I hope you realise that.'

For the second morning in a row, Tracy and Holly had dragged Belinda out of her warm bed, and Belinda was not pleased.

They were standing on the platform at Mosley, huddled in their coats and waiting for a train.

'You don't get pneumonia from snow,' said Tracy. 'Don't be such a wimp.'

Belinda shivered. 'You'll see,' she said. 'And when you're lying in your hospital beds, half dead with *triple*-pneumonia, I hope you'll remember that I warned you.'

'We'll remember,' said Holly. 'You'll be able to say, I told you so, OK? But meanwhile we've got to find Jamie and wring his neck.'

'He's a persistent little devil, isn't he?' said Tracy. She looked at Holly. 'It was a bit dumb of you to leave our notebook lying around where he could find it, though, don't you think?'

Holly glared at her. 'Thanks,' she said. 'I'll remember that in future.' It didn't help calm Holly's temper that her two friends seemed to think it was her fault that Jamie had been able to get at their notes about Oliver Duke.

It wasn't long before the train came rattling and rumbling into the station.

'What exactly do you plan to do?' asked Belinda, as the train carried them off towards Lychthorpe. 'He's got quite a head start on us, hasn't he?'

'That's true,' said Tracy. 'He could have been to the book shop, gotten the book, and vanished with it before we even arrive.'

'He won't have *vanished*,' said Holly. 'He'll be around somewhere.'

'Hmm,' said Belinda. 'Following up the clues.'

'If he can figure them out,' said Holly. 'If you ask me, Philip is the real brains behind that pair. Jamie couldn't have worked it out on his own. And now he *is* on his own, trying to use his peanut-sized brain to guess what that book is all about.' She gave her friends a grim smile. 'We'll find him,' she said. 'We'll find him, get the book off him, and then kill him.'

They came into Gilchrist's bookshop to find the old shopkeeper balanced precariously at the top of a rickety step-ladder, hefting a pile of books up on to a high shelf.

Tracy ran forwards and held the steps, while the grey-haired man climbed down.

'They don't look too safe,' she said. 'You want to be careful you don't have an accident.'

He gave her one of his crocodile smiles. 'You're

probably right,' he said. 'If I were keeping the shop on, I'd invest in a new stepladder.' He rubbed his hands together. 'You've been pipped at the post, I'm afraid,' he said.

'We've been what?' asked Tracy.

'The young gentleman was here when I opened up this morning,' explained the shopkeeper. 'I must say, he's done very well with his research. I've got to admit, I never expected to see any of you again, but the young gentleman had got all the details I needed to be able to find the book.'

'*He* didn't get them,' exclaimed Holly. '*We* did. We spoke to the vicar yesterday, but Jamie stole my notes.'

The shopkeeper frowned. 'Well, I don't call that very sporting of him,' he said. 'That's not playing the game at all.'

'But you sold him the book?' asked Belinda.

'Of course,' said the shopkeeper. 'I wasn't to know how he'd found out about it.' He shook his head. 'I'm very sorry if he's beaten you by unfair means, young ladies,' he said. 'I'd never have given it to him if I'd known he had cheated. But I'm sure that the organisers of the competition will disqualify him once you tell them how he's behaved.'

The shopkeeper clearly still thought they were searching for the book as part of some treasure hunt. He'd said something of the sort yesterday, and the girls hadn't told him otherwise.

'I don't suppose you've got two copies of the book?' asked Holly.

The shopkeeper shook his head. 'I'm afraid not,' he said. 'It's a very old book – but not the sort that ever became valuable. Goodness knows how long it's been in stock.'

'Can you tell us anything about it?' asked Belinda.

'It is an eighteenth century anthology of poetry,' said the shopkeeper. 'It's only a slim volume. A collection of poems written by people who lived in Lychthorpe in those days. Published at his own expense by the local doctor, according to the preface. I doubt that there were ever more than a couple of dozen copies printed.' He smiled at them. 'I'm afraid it didn't appear to include anything of particular merit, from the brief glance I had at it. The doctor who published it included several of his own poems.' He pulled a face. 'Not terribly good poems, I'm afraid. I think he included poems by other people just to pad it out a bit.'

'Including one by Oliver Duke?' said Holly.

'That's right,' said the shopkeeper. 'That's how I was able to track it down. Once your young friend had given me the name of Oliver Duke, I was able to go through my files. The man who owned this shop before me was particularly interested in poetry, and he'd cross-referenced all the names – even to the extent of people as obscure as your Mr Duke.'

'And now Jamie's got it!' exclaimed Holly. The shopkeeper looked unhappily at her. 'Oh, well,' she said. 'It can't be helped.' She gave him a forlorn smile. 'Thanks, anyway,' she said. 'It's not your fault that my brother is such a cheat.'

They left the shop.

'Well?' said Belinda. 'What's the plan now?'

'Mystery Club meeting,' said Holly. She pointed over towards the green. 'We've got to think about this.'

They gathered on the bench in the middle of the green.

'What are we planning?' asked Belinda. 'Methods of killing Jamie?'

'Eventually,' said Holly. 'But we need to find him first.'

'If you ask me,' said Tracy, 'he's not going to be far away. Everything seems to have gone on in this village. Oliver Duke lived here. The book was published here. It all points to the amulet being hidden somewhere nearby.' She looked at her friends. 'Don't you agree?'

'That makes sense,' said Belinda. 'Except that the vicar thought the amulet had already been found. By Oliver Duke's daughter.'

'That Tessa woman obviously doesn't think so,' said Holly.

'True,' said Belinda. She looked at Holly. 'What do you think Jamie would do?'

'He'd go somewhere quiet to read the poem,' said Holly. 'Then he'd follow up the clues, if there are any.'

'Tessa seemed pretty certain the poem would lead to the amulet,' said Tracy. 'The only question is whether Jamie could figure it out.'

'And if he can't?' asked Belinda.

'He'd go back to Philip's place,' said Holly. 'Like I said, Philip's got all the brain cells between them. He'd go back there and get Philip to read it.'

'Right,' said Belinda. 'I think we should split up. One of us to go back to the station and see if he's been seen getting a train, and the other two to have a good look round the village, in case he's still lurking about somewhere.'

Belinda's plan seemed like their only way forward. There was certainly nothing else they could do in Lychthorpe without finding Jamie first.

'And whoever finds him,' said Holly, 'get that blessed book off him any way you can. If Tessa does what she said she was going to do, she's going to be arriving at the station here at a quarter to four. The best thing we can do is be there waiting for her, and give her the book.' She grinned. 'It'll involve some explaining, but I'm sure we can manage that. OK,' finished Holly 'let's go.'

'Message received and understood,' said Tracy with a grin. 'Let's go for it, you guys. Operation: Get Jamie Adams!'

Belinda headed back to the station.

'I'll come with you,' said Holly. 'Jamie might have gone over to the church. He knew we'd got all our information from the vicar there. He might go there himself.'

'And I'll go look around near that pub,' said Tracy. 'We'll meet up at the station in, say, half an hour. We'll have been able to go right through this place in that time.'

As Tracy crossed the road towards the sidestreet where they had seen the boarded-up pub, she felt something cold touch her cheek. A single drifting snowflake.

They never had snow in California where she had been brought up, and she still found the idea of snow romantic – although she preferred to see it through the window of a warm room. English winters might look pretty on Christmas cards, but they were not much fun to be out in.

Tracy drew her coat closer, looking up to see the heavy grey sky dotted with slowly falling snowflakes.

It's hardly a blizzard, she thought, thankfully.

But the sooner we find Jamie and head off home, the happier I'll be.

She thrust her hands into her coat pockets. The Duke Oliver was as deserted as ever. The portrait of the highwayman stared menacingly down at her, his two pistols seemingly aimed straight at her as his eyes gleamed behind his mask.

She shivered at the thought of the old days, when men such as Oliver Duke prowled the highways and byways of the area, robbing passers-by at gunpoint. And to think that he had managed to fool the people into believing he was just the landlord of their local pub!

There was a narrow alley alongside the pub. Tracy walked down it, ready to give Jamie a good piece of her mind if she did happen upon him.

But it wasn't Jamie that she saw as she came to the end of the alley and out into an open area behind the pub. Ahead of her was a rusted wire fence that bordered the railway line. Off to her left she could see the edge of the station platform. But parked a little way off, up against the fence, was a white van.

Tracy ducked back around the edge of the pub's rear wall. It was Tony Blake's van. She was sure of it. She'd seen it the other day, parked outside Holly's house.

In their desire to track Jamie down, the three friends had almost forgotten about Tony Blake – or at least, they had assumed he had gone away after encountering them the previous day. But here was his van again. Hidden away behind the pub.

Tracy glanced around the corner of the wall.

Was he in the van? There was certainly no sign of anyone in the front – but Jamie and Philip had said they'd disturbed him *sleeping* in it. Could he be in the back?

It was impossible to tell from that distance. Tracy gnawed her bottom lip. There was something very peculiar about the van still being there. And the only way she could think to try and find out *why* it was still there was to go over and have a closer look.

After all, she thought, *even if he is there, what can he do?*

She slipped out of cover and walked slowly over to the van.

Silent as a mouse, she peered through the window on the passenger's side. It was open a few centimetres. On the seat she saw some empty take-away food cartons and a couple of open drink cans. Someone had been in this van long enough to need food and drink.

She crept to the back. The two rear doors to the van had small square windows set in them. She leaned closer to look through. Her heart gave a little leap. Curled on a blanket in the back of the van was Tony Blake's alsatian. Fortunately it seemed to be deeply asleep.

But something else lay in the back of the van. A long, narrow leather case, wider at one end than at the other, with a strap for carrying it.

Tracy's eyes widened. She couldn't be sure, but she had the dreadful feeling that she recognised what that case was. Back in California she had seen cases just like that. She had never seen one in England, but in America such cases were used to hold hunting rifles.

The appearance of the van took on a new menace. If she was right, why would Tony Blake have a rifle with him?

She took another look, trying to see better, hoping that her first impressions of the case had been wrong. Perhaps it held something completely innocent, and she was letting her imagination run away with her. Perhaps it held nothing more dangerous than a dismantled fishing rod or a snooker cue?

There was a movement from inside the van. The alsatian's head lifted and Tracy found herself staring into its open dark eyes.

'Good boy,' she whispered. 'Don't worry. I'm not doing anything. There's a good boy.'

The dog scrambled to its feet and sprang towards

the back of the van, barking wildly and scrabbling at the back doors.

Tracy jumped back, alarmed by the noise the dog was making. She stared round, fearing to see Tony Blake appear in response to the dog's barking.

The van shook from the impact of the dog's claws on the back doors. It looked almost big enough and ferocious enough to burst them open and leap out at her.

She hesitated for a moment, then ran towards the alley, hoping that Tony Blake was far enough away for her to escape with her startling news. To get back to Holly and Belinda without him discovering her.

There was no sign of the friendly vicar, or of anyone else, for that matter, as Holly approached the old church. A few flakes of snow floated down out of the sky, settling for an instant on the path before melting away.

'Jamie!' she shouted, her voice ringing out loudly in the silence. 'Are you hiding?'

There was no response, but then she hadn't really expected one. If Jamie was somewhere nearby, he'd be more likely to go into deeper cover if he heard her voice. He wasn't so silly that he wouldn't know the sort of reception he'd get if she found him. She had really only shouted to relieve the silence – the close proximity of the ancient graveyard was working on her imagination, sending shivers up and down her spine.

Holly walked through the churchyard, circling the solid old building. She had noticed that the front doors were locked shut. She glanced over the back wall to the old oak tree where Oliver Duke was buried in his unmarked grave.

A sudden sound broke faintly in the strange silence. Someone was hammering. A deep, echoing thudding noise.

Holly walked along the back of the church, trying to pinpoint the direction from which the sound was coming.

Away to her right were a couple of old wooden sheds. The thumping noise seemed to be coming from there.

'Hello?' she shouted. 'Is there anyone there?'

'Holly?' came a muffled response. 'Holly? It's *me*! Help.'

It was Jamie's voice.

'Jamie?' Holly ran forwards. The door to one of the sheds shook as she heard the sound of more thumping.

'Jamie? What on earth are you doing in there?' shouted Holly. The door was padlocked.

'Get me out!' shouted Jamie. 'He locked me in here! He stole the book off me and locked me in here!'

'Who did?' gasped Holly. 'Jamie? What are you talking about? Who locked you in here?'

'*He* did,' shouted Jamie. 'The man with the dog. Tony Blake! Tony Blake did it!'

6   Rhyming clues

'Get me out of here!' shouted Jamie, hammering again on the inside of the shed door. 'Holly? What are you playing at?'

'It's padlocked,' said Holly. 'I'm looking for something to . . . *ah!*' At the side of the shed she spotted a pile of stone pieces that looked like broken-up chunks of gravestones.

'Just a second,' she called. She lifted a large square stone in her hands. 'Stand back!' she panted, her legs buckling under the weight.

She tensed her arm muscles and toppled the stone forwards against the door. There was a crack and a wrenching sound. Holly jumped back as the stone thudded to the ground.

'Got it!' she said. The impact of the stone had torn the hasp loose and it was only a matter of a few jerks before it came away in her hand.

Pushed from the inside, the door sprang open a few centimetres before it hit against the fallen stone.

'Ow!' she heard Jamie cry. 'My nose!'

Holly dragged the stone away and pulled the door open.

Jamie was standing there, holding his nose.

'You idiot!' he said. 'What did you do that for? I've broken my nose!' He took his hand away. 'Is there any blood?'

'Not a drop,' said Holly. 'You should have waited until I'd moved the stone out of the way. Let me see.' She prodded Jamie's nose and he let out a howl of protest.

'Give over,' said Holly. 'There's nothing wrong with it. Now, what's all this about Tony Blake?'

Jamie gave an experimental sniff. 'He locked me in here,' he said. 'He took the book and locked me in this shed.'

Holly stared at him. 'What on earth for?' She frowned suspiciously at Jamie. 'Are you playing one of your stupid jokes on me?'

'Oh, yes,' said Jamie caustically. 'I suppose I locked myself in here, did I?'

'No,' admitted Holly. 'I suppose not. Look, what exactly happened?'

'I got the book from that weird old man in the bookshop,' said Jamie. 'I found the poem by that highwayman.' He looked at Holly. 'It's the stupidest poem I've ever read,' he said. 'I couldn't understand a word of it.'

'Never mind that for now,' said Holly. 'Tell me about Tony Blake.'

'I was going to get a train back and show the poem to Philip,' said Jamie. 'He's cleverer than I am at figuring these things out. I was just crossing the railway when I saw that Blake man following me. So I ran for it. He ran after me.' He gave his sister a fierce look. 'Didn't I tell you he was after that amulet? Didn't I say that all along?'

'Yes,' said Holly. 'You did. So, what happened then?'

'I ran over here. I thought I'd be able to circle round and lose him,' said Jamie. 'But he's quicker than he looks. He caught me and swiped the book off me. I started to yell for help and the next thing I knew he'd shoved me in this shed and locked the door on me.'

'Did he hurt you?' asked Holly.

'No,' said Jamie, carefully touching his nose again. *'You're* the one who hurt me. He just stole my book, the rotten pig!'

'We've got to get the police,' said Holly. 'I don't know what Tony Blake thinks he's up to, but he can't be allowed to get away with *this*.' She grabbed Jamie's arm and marched him back around to the front of the church. 'Belinda is at the railway station. We'll pick her up there and ask the way to the police station.'

They found Belinda standing huddled in her coat by the level-crossing.

'Aha!' she shouted. 'You got him! Good! Where's

the book?'

Her jaw fell open as Holly explained what had happened.

'You're joking?' she gasped. 'Tony Blake is still hanging around here? Crumbs, he must really think that amulet is worth a fortune if he's prepared to go to these lengths.'

'I don't care what he believes,' said Holly. 'I'm getting the police.'

They looked round at the sound of a high-pitched shout from the other side of the railway. It was Tracy. With a wave, she came running over the level-crossing.

'You're not going to believe what I've seen!' she panted.

'Tony Blake?' said Holly.

Tracy came to a skidding halt. 'What! No – his van,' she said in surprise. 'But how—'

'He locked Jamie up round the back of the church and stole the book,' explained Holly. 'Where was the van?'

'In a sort of carpark in back of the pub,' said Tracy. 'That dog was in there, but the Blake guy wasn't around.'

'He's around here somewhere,' said Belinda. 'What do we do? Call the police?'

'No,' said Holly. 'Let's see if we can find him, first. Then one of us can keep tabs on him while the others get the police.'

'If you think so,' said Tracy. 'But there's something else. I could be wrong, but I saw something in the back of his van that looked like the sort of case people carry rifles around in.'

'Are you *sure* about that?' said Belinda.

'Well, no,' admitted Tracy. 'I only got a quick look before that darned dog of his started barking at me.'

'Let's go and look,' said Holly. She looked at Jamie. 'I think you'd better stay here,' she said.

'No way!' said Jamie. 'If that creep's going to get caught, I want to be in on it.'

'We're not going to *catch* him,' said Holly. 'In fact, we're going to make sure he doesn't see us. But you can come along, if you must. Just keep out of sight, that's all.'

The snow was beginning to fall more thickly now, white curtains trailing down from the sky as they made their way towards the street with The Duke Oliver pub in it.

Cautiously, and in single file, with Tracy at the head, they crept along the alleyway.

She stopped suddenly and the others bumped into her.

'What?' whispered Holly.

'Shhh!' hissed Tracy. 'He's *there*!'

Holly looked round her friend's shoulder. On the far side of the otherwise empty carpark she could see Tony Blake's white van. And through the side window she could see a dark shape sitting at the wheel.

'What's he doing?' whispered Belinda.

'I can't see,' said Holly. 'He's just sitting there.'

'I think he's reading something,' said Tracy.

'My book!' said Jamie. 'I bet it is!'

'Quiet!' whispered Holly. But it was too late. Either by some acute animal sense, or from the faint sound of their voices magnified by its sensitive hearing, the alsatian had become alerted to their presence.

It began to bark from the back of the van. Tracy saw Tony Blake's head snap round. He stared straight at them for an instant, a look of surprised anger on his face. Then he gunned the van's engine and the vehicle went speeding away over the tarmac in a squeal of tyres.

It vanished alongside the wire fence, driving along a narrow roadway behind the other buildings.

Tracy ran forward in time to see the van take a sharp right turn at the end of the tarmac path.

'That was your fault!' Holly yelled at Jamie.

'It never was,' said Jamie. 'If Tracy hadn't stuck her big head out he wouldn't have seen us.'

'Well,' said Belinda, 'he's gone now. We might as well find the police station. There's no point in hanging round here. He's not going to be coming back now he knows we've spotted him.'

'I guess so,' sighed Tracy.

The three girls started to walk back down the alley. Holly looked round. Jamie was standing watching them with his arms folded.

'What are you doing, Jamie?' she called.

'I can't believe my eyes,' he said, his voice dripping with sarcasm. 'Are you three giving up the race, then?'

'What race?' asked Belinda. She looked at Holly. 'What's the little twerp talking about?'

'The *amulet*,' said Jamie. 'I thought we were here to find that amulet?'

Holly stared at him. 'It may have escaped your notice, pea-brain,' she said, 'but even if we wanted to carry on looking for this precious amulet of yours, after what's been going on this morning, we *can't*.'

'Can't we?' said Jamie. 'Why not?'

'He's stolen the book with the poem in it, dim-wit,' said Holly.

'But I copied the poem out,' said Jamie with one of his irritating smirks. 'I've got it written down.' He pulled a crumpled piece of paper out of his pocket. 'See?'

'Why didn't you say so?' said Holly.

Jamie grinned. 'You never asked. Anyway, I wasn't going to just hand it over to you. Look, why don't we join forces? I don't mind admitting that I can't make any sense of the poem, but if

87

you're prepared to agree that I won the race for the book, then I'll show it to you and we can look for the amulet together. What do you say?'

'I say we get the police,' said Belinda.

'No, wait,' said Tracy. 'The kid's got a point. Blake has gone, right? He's no immediate problem now, but he does have the poem. While we're talking to the police he's going to be looking for the amulet.'

Belinda looked at Holly, seeing that familiar gleam in her eyes. The gleam that always seemed to lead to trouble.

'Now, look here . . .' Belinda began forlornly.

'Show me,' Holly said to Jamie. She looked round at her friends. 'At least we could have a look at it, couldn't we?' she said.

Belinda looked at Tracy for support, but Tracy's face showed the same eagerness as Holly's.

'Oh, well,' sighed Belinda. 'Here we go again.'

The three girls gathered around Jamie. He had scribbled the poem on the back of one of the sheets that he'd torn out of the Mystery Club's notebook.

'By the way,' Holly said to Jamie. 'Remind me to *kill* you when this is all over, for tearing those pages out of our notebook.'

Jamie grinned at her. 'You'll forget all about that,' he said, 'when we find the amulet.'

'I doubt it,' said Holly. 'Come on, show us the

poem, then.'

Jamie handed her the crumpled sheet of paper.

'See what I mean?' he said. 'It's just a lot of nonsense.'

They read the scribbled poem:

Sir Toby is filled with ale to the brim
But his voice never slurs, nor eyesight grows dim.
As soon as he's empty he'll always take more.
He sits on the shelf and he watches the floor.

A tun or a keg, a butt or a cask,
Sir Toby he knows, you have only to ask.
A firkin, a puncheon, a vat or hogshead,
Old Toby he sees, but he's dumb as the dead.

So knock on wood, hark, and along you will go,
To where five strikes four, above from below.
May luck not desert you, nor senses grow frail.
Remember Sir Toby and give him some ale.

The girls looked at one another.

'Sir *Toby*?' said Tracy. 'Who the heck is Sir Toby? Some guy who used to drink in the pub?'

'Whoever he was,' said Belinda, 'it looks like he knew where the amulet was hidden. Assuming, of course, that this poem really is a clue.'

'Of course it is,' said Holly. 'Look: *Sir Toby he knows, You have only to ask.* That's pretty clear, isn't it?'

'But this Toby guy would have died a couple of hundred years ago,' said Tracy. 'So how are

89

we supposed to ask him *anything*? And what do these other words mean? *A firkin, a puncheon, a vat or hogshead*?'

Holly frowned. 'I know the word "firkin" from somewhere,' she said. 'And a vat is just a big water container.'

Belinda gave them a grin. 'Let me know when you've got bored with guessing, and I'll tell you,' she said.

'Don't be smug, Belinda,' said Tracy. 'You know what they say: pride comes before a fall.'

'They're all containers for beer,' explained Belinda. 'Different sized barrels. Firkins and kegs are the little ones. If I remember correctly, a hogshead holds about two hundred litres.' She closed one eye and tilted her head as she tried to remember. 'A butt holds twice as much as a hogshead. And I think a tun is the biggest of the lot.' Her mouth spread in a grin that threatened to meet around the back of her head. 'And the next question, please.'

'The next question is: what did Oliver Duke think he was going on about?' said Jamie.

'It must be something to do with the pub,' said Tracy. She looked up at the wall of the empty building. 'It's a pity we can't get in there and have a look round.'

Jamie walked to the back end of the alley. 'Look,' he said. 'Couldn't we get this open?'

At the back of the pub, close up against the wall,

a wooden trapdoor was set into the ground. The only other way in was through a heavy old door that didn't look as if it had been opened for years.

'It must be the way down into the cellar,' said Belinda, looking at the trapdoor. 'There'd be a chute under there, and they'd roll the barrels down to be stored.'

Holly knelt by the trapdoor. 'The question is,' she said, running a hand over the rough old wood, 'how do we get it open? There's no handle or hand-hole on the outside.'

'Of course there isn't,' said Belinda. 'Or anyone could get in. These things only open from the inside, and they're locked shut with bolts.' She shook her head. 'You'll never get it open.' She pointed up at a small window set well above head-height in the back wall. 'That's our best bet, if you ask me,' she said.

Tracy eyed the narrow window. 'I could get up there,' she said. 'If someone gave me a leg up. But I don't know if I could get through, even if it can be opened. It looks kind of a tight fit.'

'I could do it, easy,' said Jamie.

'Yes,' said Holly. 'And fall through and break your neck.'

'Got any better suggestions?' asked Jamie. 'I want to have a look inside, even if you lot don't.' He looked at Holly with shining eyes. 'You never know,' he said. 'The amulet might be hidden in there.'

'OK,' said Holly. 'You win. But if you *do* break your neck, remember I told you so.'

Holly stood under the window with her back to the wall. She cupped her hands into a stirrup and, with Tracy's help, Jamie managed to clamber awkwardly up until his feet were on her shoulders and the sill of the window was at his chest level.

'Can you get it open?' groaned Holly as her brother's shoes ground into her shoulders. 'Jamie? Don't take all day about it.'

'Hold on,' called Jamie. 'I – *oops!*' There was a dry crack of wood, followed a second later by a dull crash from inside the pub. The entire window had caved in at his touch, the wooden frame rotted away by years of exposure to the weather.

'That's one way of getting it open,' Belinda remarked drily. '*Very* subtle.'

'Can you get through?' asked Tracy, still holding Jamie's legs as he wobbled on Holly's aching shoulders.

'Yes. I think so,' said Jamie.

'Ouch!' yelled Holly as the heel of Jamie's shoe clipped her head. 'That was my ear!'

As Jamie's rear end disappeared through the window, Holly distinctly heard him giggling to himself.

The three girls gathered at the door. It wasn't

long before they heard noises from inside. The sound of Jamie wrestling with rusty old bolts.

'At least he didn't break his neck,' said Tracy.

'No,' said Holly, rubbing her stinging ear. 'Pity.' With a screech of hinges the door opened inwards and a dusty Jamie stood grinning at them.

They came into an entrance lobby, from which led several doors and a staircase to the next floor. Wallpaper hung off in mouldy strips and the carpet was filthy beneath their feet.

They tried the doors. A couple of cupboards, a dingy kitchen and another room with abandoned pieces of furniture and other rubbish in it.

'This is the way to the public part,' said Belinda, opening a door into a large room. It had dark brown paint on the woodwork and ceiling, and gloomy red flock wallpaper on the walls. They walked into the long, L-shaped room, a musty, cold odour greeting them. There were leather seats against the walls, and round iron tables with stained tops. A long, curved bar wound itself along one side of the room.

Light filtered through dirt-encrusted bottle-glass windows.

Belinda lifted a flap at one end of the bar and walked behind. Beer pumps stood in groups of three.

'Anyone for a quick drink?' she asked, pulling one of the levers. There was a dry rasp from the pump. 'Oh, well, perhaps not,' she said. The shelves behind the bar were thick with dust. She wrote her name in the dust on the bar top. 'Well?' she said. 'Now what?'

'Search,' said Jamie. 'Everywhere. Turn the whole place over.'

'It'll take for ever,' said Holly. 'Let's *think* first, shall we? What did the poem say, again?' She smoothed the sheet of paper out on the bar top.

While the three girls re-read it, Jamie wandered around the long, crooked room, peering into nooks and under the benches as if he expected the amulet just to be lying around somewhere.

Tracy roved her eyes over the shelves behind the bar. They were empty of anything but dust – except in one corner, where something caught her eye. For a second she couldn't make it out. It looked like a face.

'We're being watched,' she said. 'Look.'

The others turned to follow the line of her eyes. It was a large china mug, sitting alone on a shelf, its outer surface moulded into the shape of a face. A face with fat red cheeks and a large moustache.

'He looks a happy kind of guy,' Tracy said.

'It's a toby jug,' Belinda said excitedly. She looked at the others. 'Sir *Toby*! That's what the poem meant. *Sir Toby is filled with ale to the brim*! It didn't mean a person. Oliver Duke was writing about a toby jug.' She ran over to the jug and reached up to take it down. But it was fixed to the shelf.

'Perhaps there's something inside?' said Holly.

Using the lower shelves as steps, Belinda lifted herself and looked into the jug.

'Rats!' she said. 'It's empty.'

'Wait,' said Holly. 'It says: *he sits on the shelf and watches the floor*. Is there anything on the floor over there, Belinda?'

Belinda jumped down, her feet echoing hollowly. 'I'll say there is,' she said. 'Another trapdoor. Right here.'

'Jamie,' called Holly. 'Come on, we've found something.'

The three of them joined Belinda behind the bar. She was kneeling, brushing dust and dirt away from a metal handle set flat into the face of the trapdoor.

'It means the cellar,' said Belinda. 'The poem must mean you should look in the cellar. Of course! That's where all the barrels would be.'

'The amulet must be hidden in one of the barrels,' said Jamie. 'Come on! What are you waiting for? Get it open!'

Belinda managed to prise the stiff handle up. She braced herself and gave a heave. The trapdoor opened couple of centimetres then thudded down again in a puff of dust.

'It's too heavy,' she said.

'Let me,' said Tracy. Although lighter and more slender than Belinda, Tracy's sporting activities gave her an edge over her friend.

She gripped the handle and slowly heaved it open.

'Grab hold,' she said.

Several pairs of hands caught hold of the raised trapdoor and it came crashing open, revealing a dark hole. Narrow, wooden steps led down into the darkness.

The girls looked at one another.

'Well?' said Holly. 'Who wants to try it?'

'Its pretty dark down there,' said Tracy. 'Ugh! And it smells bad.' A waft of fetid air blew up out of the hole. 'Count me out,' she said.

'Cowards!' said Jamie. 'I'm not scared of an old cellar.'

'It's not a case of being scared, Jamie,' said Holly. 'We won't be able to see anything.'

'I'm going to try it anyway,' said Jamie. He stretched a foot into the hole and stamped experimentally on the top step. 'No problems,' he said. Turning to face the steep steps he lowered himself into the square hole. He grinned up at the anxious faces of the girls.

'See?' he said smugly. 'It's as safe as—.' A look of alarm crossed his face as one of the lower steps snapped suddenly under his probing foot.

'Jamie!' Holly cried in fright as her brother grabbed in panic at the sides of the hole.

There was nothing they could do. It all happened too quickly. One second he was staring up at them, and the next second there was a crash of timbers as he vanished down out of sight.

'Jamie!' screamed Holly, as a cloud of dust rose up out of the hole. 'Jamie? Are you all right?'

7   Knock on wood

Holly leaned into the square hole in the floor, trying to see down through the darkness and the rising dust. She was leaning over perilously far.

'Jamie?' she called.

'Careful,' said Tracy, catching a hold around Holly's waist to save her from following her brother into the black gulf.

'Can you see anything?' asked Belinda.

Holly strained her eyes. There was something visible through the billows of dust.

'Jamie? Are you hurt?' she shouted. She gave Belinda a panicked look. 'What am I going to tell Mum?' she said.

'Holly?' Jamie's voice came wavering up. The three girls breathed a collective sigh of relief.

'Are you hurt?' called Holly.

'Yes,' Jamie shouted up. 'I think I've broken my leg.'

'Oh, no!' cried Holly.

'And my arm,' shouted Jamie. 'And my other arm. Oh, and my other leg as well.' His face appeared suddenly through the dust. He was grinning. 'And my neck,' he said. 'And I'm pretty sure I've got a fractured skull.' He clung to the steps, his hair all standing up on end. 'Were you worried?'

'You . . . you . . .' Words failed Holly. 'I wish you *had* broken your neck!' she exclaimed. 'At least then you wouldn't have been any more trouble.'

Belinda laughed. 'I think it makes a nice change,' she said. 'It's usually me that does things like that.'

As the dust settled and their eyes became accustomed to the gloom, they could see the broken tread that had caused Jamie's fall.

'I landed on a load of old cardboard boxes,' he explained. 'Just like in films. You know, when stuntmen chuck themselves off buildings.'

'We need a light if we're going down there safely,' said Tracy. 'A torch or something.'

'Hold on,' said Belinda, scrambling to her feet. 'I think I saw something in the kitchen that might be useful. You stay here, I shan't be a moment.'

She went back into the entrance lobby and opened the kitchen door. The room was lit dimly by light that filtered in through the boarded-up window.

'Yes!' she said to herself. 'I thought so.' A few abandoned odds and ends lay on a heavy wooden table. Among the rubbish stood a hurricane-lamp.

She walked over to the table and picked up the lamp. She heard the swish of paraffin from inside. Now all she needed was something with which to light it.

She searched the room, opening drawers and cupboards.

'Aha!' In one of the cupboards she found a box half-filled with books of matches. The flaps were decorated with the masked face of the highwayman. 'That's *exactly* what we need,' she said.

It took her a little while to get the old lamp working, as she pumped the handle to bring the fuel up to the wick. Half a dozen matches later the lamp was giving out a powerful white light.

As she carried the lamp back to the others she paused, hearing a sound from outside. An unpleasantly familiar sound. The single bark of a dog.

They had closed the back door behind themselves. Belinda didn't want to risk opening it and being seen. She crouched and lifted the flap of the letterbox. Through the oblong hole she could see the falling snow. But nothing else. The dog had only barked once, but she was in no doubt that it was Tony Blake's alsatian.

She made her way back to the others.

'I don't want to worry you,' she said. 'But I think Blake's come back.'

'Let's get out of here,' said Holly. 'I don't want to meet up with him.'

'No way,' Tracy said determinedly. 'We're too close to finding that amulet. If we go down to the cellar and close the trapdoor, he's not going to know we're even here. And if he does figure it out, we can always escape through that other trapdoor out the back. The one Belinda said opens from inside.'

'Right!' said Jamie. 'Let's get on with it, then.'

Carefully avoiding the broken tread, Tracy made her way down the steps while Belinda shone the light from above.

Holly lifted the trapdoor as Belinda followed Tracy. Supporting the weight of the trapdoor against one arm, Holly made her cautious way down the steps. The trapdoor closed with a dull thud.

The cellar proved to be not one room, but a series of small rooms that led into one another, divided by solid, brick walls hanging with cobwebs.

'Brrr,' murmured Belinda, shivering despite her coat. 'It's like an icebox down here.' She swung the lamp, revealing murky corners. Their shadows leaped eerily over the filthy walls. 'Where do you suggest we start searching?'

They huddled together, baffled by the number of rooms. The air was foul and chillingly damp.

'The poem was all about barrels,' said Holly.

'There are plenty of those around,' said Tracy. Half a dozen small wooden barrels were stacked

101

against the wall, and through the doorways they could see crates and discarded bottles in other rooms.

'But what about the third verse?' said Belinda. 'The bit about knocking on wood. What's that all about?'

'*So knock on wood, hark, and through you will go,*' read Holly. 'What do you think that means?'

'It must mean we should knock on the barrels,' said Belinda. 'Oliver Duke wouldn't have hidden the amulet in a full barrel, would he? And empty barrels will make a different sound to full ones.'

Jamie spotted something lying in a corner. He went over and picked it up. It was a black, iron jemmy.

'We can break them open with this,' he said. 'Watch!' He grasped the jemmy in both hands and swung it at one of the small barrels. It bounced off without effect, giving out a dull thud.

'You'll never break into them like that,' said Tracy. 'They're too strong. We'll have to try prising the lids off.'

They gathered around one of the barrels, holding it steady while Jamie jammed the end of the jemmy into the top and pushed down with all his weight.

There was a sharp crack as the metal hoop holding the barrel together snapped. They jumped back as a dark flood of ancient beer spilled out over the floor.

'I think we're on the wrong track, you know,' said Holly as they moved back to avoid the foamy puddles. 'It says, knock on wood, listen and *through* you will go. It doesn't say anything about finding something *in* a barrel.'

'But how do you go *through* a barrel?' asked Tracy. 'It doesn't make any sense.'

'It might do if it was a big enough barrel,' said Belinda.

'OK,' said Jamie, hefting the jemmy on to his shoulder. 'Let's look for some bigger barrels.'

They passed through into another of the underground chambers. There were wine racks and a few broken bottles on the floor. But in the room beyond, they saw what they were looking for. Lying in a row against the wall were four enormous barrels.

Jamie hit the jemmy against the lid of the first one.

'That sounds full,' said Belinda. 'Careful with that thing, Jamie. If you break one of these we're going to be swimming in beer.'

Jamie struck the next barrel along. A hollow boom echoed around the room.

'Did you hear that?' said Tracy. 'It's empty!'

'We've found it!' Jamie said excitedly. 'Give me a hand.'

Together, Holly and Jamie managed to force the flat end of the jemmy in under the edge of the broad lid. They heaved, feeling the lid give a little.

With a startling suddenness, the heavy lid toppled forward and thudded to the floor.

Belinda lifted the lamp, shining it into the mouth of the barrel. She looked around at the others, her eyes gleaming behind her glasses. 'There's no back to it,' she said. 'Look. I can see the wall.'

They crowded around her. Sure enough, where they had expected to see the wooden end of the barrel, they could see rough brickwork.

'It's just a fake,' said Tracy. She crawled into the barrel. 'Give me the lamp,' she said.

She held the lamp out in front of her, kneeling in the confined space. A large spider crawled away between two bricks.

'Well?' said Holly, leaning into the barrel. 'See anything?'

Tracy ran her fingers over the bricks. They felt cold and damp and unpleasant. Her fingers hit against a brick standing proud of the others. Putting the lamp down, she took hold of the brick. She had expected some resistance, and she was taken by surprise when the brick slid out in her hands. She fell backwards with a yell, the loose brick in her hands.

'It's a hidey-hole!' said Belinda. She stared at the eager faces of the others. 'I don't believe it,' she said. 'We've actually *found* it!'

Tracy sat up.

'Feel in the hole,' said Holly.

'OK, OK, give me a second,' said Tracy. She ran her hand around the black hole. 'There are more loose bricks,' she said.

'Can you see the amulet?' said Jamie, pushing past Holly and Belinda and crawling into the barrel.

'No. I can't see anything,' said Tracy. 'Jamie! Get out of the way, will you?' As she moved to try and avoid Jamie, she slipped and fell against the wall. There was a rush and a crash as the bricks gave way under her and she found herself sprawling into a large dark hole.

Jamie lifted the lamp. 'Wow!' he said softly. 'It's a tunnel.' The light revealed a long, low-roofed tunnel that stretched itself away into the distance. It was no more than a metre high, supported at intervals by wooden beams, its floor, walls and ceiling of dark tight-packed earth. Here and there roots had broken through and white mould shone in wet patches.

'Where do you think it leads?' said Belinda.

Tracy sat up, brushing brick dust out of her hair, the sleeves of her coat smeared with wet earth. She glared at Jamie. 'Look what you did!' she said. 'I'm filthy.'

'I was only trying to help,' said Jamie. 'I don't know what you're complaining about. I found the tunnel, didn't I?'

'Oliver Duke must have used it to get in and

out of the pub without being seen,' Holly breathed excitedly. 'When he was off being a highwayman. Do you think—'

'Shhh!' hissed Belinda. 'Listen!' She had heard something. A bang from above. They became silent. An echoey creaking crept across the ceiling.

'There's someone up there,' whispered Holly. 'Someone's got into the pub.'

'Blake!' hissed Belinda. 'It *must* be.'

They listened as the soft creaking moved across the wooden boards of the ceiling. Dust filtered down.

'He won't come down here, will he?' Jamie whispered hopefully. 'He can't know we're here.'

'He may not know *we're* here,' hissed Belinda. 'But he's got the poem, hasn't he? If we could figure the clues out, I'm sure *he* can.'

'I think we'd better get ourselves out of here,' said Holly.

'Down the tunnel!' said Jamie.

'No way,' said Belinda. 'We can get out through the other trapdoor.'

'But the tunnel . . .' began Jamie.

'Forget it,' said Holly.

Tracy pushed Jamie out of the barrel and the four of them crept through the cellars in search of the trapdoor that would take them out into the open air.

It didn't take them long to find it, at the top of a steep wooden chute. Tracy scrambled her way up. She struggled with the bolt for a few moments then came sliding back down.

'It's no good,' she said. 'It's rusted solid. No way are we *ever* going to get it open. Not in a million years.'

The girls looked at one another. How long, thought Holly, before Blake finds the trapdoor behind the bar? The thought of him cornering them down there was not a pleasant one. If he was capable of locking Jamie up to get the book, what else might he be capable of doing?

'We can try the tunnel,' said Jamie. He stared round at the girls. 'It's worth *trying*, isn't it?'

'It's better than just waiting for him to find us,' said Tracy. 'Especially if I was right, and he *is* carrying a rifle round with him.'

Holly didn't like that reminder of Tracy's suspicions.

'OK,' she said. 'The tunnel it is.'

They ran quickly back to the room with the barrels, dreading at any moment to hear renewed sounds from above that would mean that Tony Blake had found the trapdoor.

'I'll go first,' said Tracy, taking the lamp from Belinda. She crawled into the barrel.

'Be careful,' said Holly.

Belinda followed Tracy, ducking in through the

107

round wooden mouth and crawling on all fours into the damp, earthen tunnel.

'Exciting, isn't it?' said Jamie, looking round at Holly as he followed Belinda. 'And don't forget you've got me to thank for all this.'

'I shan't,' Holly said unhappily. 'I might get round to forgiving you one day, but I certainly shan't forget it.'

'Just remember the amulet,' said Jamie. 'And remember we share whatever reward there is.'

Holly shook her head. 'You're *crazy*, Jamie,' she said. 'Absolutely crazy!'

The wet of the floor seeped through the knees of Holly's jeans as she crawled along behind the others. Every now and then she glanced back, seeing the gap in the brickwork of the wall getting darker and darker as Tracy moved forwards in a pool of white light.

Where is this tunnel going to take us? she thought. *After all these years, is it going to take us anywhere?*

Cold water dripped in her hair. Her hands were grimy and muddy from the damp, earthen floor. Hanging things brushed nastily over her face. And all the time, she was straining her ears for the sound of someone following them.

'I can hardly breathe,' gasped Belinda. 'Tracy? Can you see anything up ahead?'

'Not yet,' said Tracy. She let out a long breath. 'How long does this go on for?'

Holly looked anxiously at the wooden beams that supported the roof. They looked solid enough, but supposing one of them collapsed? She pushed such thoughts away. Things were difficult enough without inventing new problems. At some stage, surely the tunnel would start to rise? It was impossible to guess how deep they were beneath ground level, but surely, she thought, their only way out was upwards?

Despite the biting cold, Tracy had to wipe sweat out of her eyes. It was no joke, crawling along in that restricted space *and* holding the heavy lamp out in front of her.

In the distance she saw a greyness in the lamplight. She had lost any track of how far they had come. It felt to her as if they had been crawling along that horrible tunnel for hours, although in reality it could only have been a few minutes at most.

'There's something up ahead,' she gasped.

'Light?' panted Belinda. 'Please let it be light!'

'No,' came Tracy's flat voice. 'It's not light. It's . . . oh, Lord! It's a wall. It's a dead end!'

'It can't be,' said Holly. 'There's got to be a way out.'

Tracy crawled up to the wall and slumped against it with a groan. 'Take a look,' she said.

The tunnel was blocked by a wall of dark bricks.

'I give up!' said Tracy. 'We'll have to go back.'

'See if there are any loose bricks,' said Belinda. 'Come on, Tracy. This isn't like you.'

Tracy looked at her. 'My arm really aches from carrying the lamp,' she said. 'And there's hardly any air down here.'

She rested the lamp on the ground.

Belinda looked back. 'Anyone following?' she asked.

Holly shook her head. 'I can't hear anyone,' she said.

Recovering from her brief despair, Tracy felt over the wall. No bricks stood out for her to take hold of.

'Try pushing,' suggested Belinda. 'Or I'll try, if you can't manage it.'

'No,' said Tracy. 'I'll do it.'

She pressed hard against the bricks.

'It's solid,' she said. 'I – hey! Wait a second!' One of the bricks seemed to give slightly to the pressure. She shifted herself round in the tunnel and pushed harder.

With a grating sound, the brick moved inwards.

'Got it!' she said, almost laughing with relief. 'Thank heavens!' She brought all her weight to bear on the brick. It edged forwards and fell away. Tracy's arm went through the hole up to her elbow.

'Hey!' she said. 'I can feel something.' Through

the hole, her hand had come into contact with something smooth and very cold. She scrabbled blindly at it with her fingers. A flat, smooth oblong, about the size of a large postcard.

She closed her fingers around it and drew her arm out. The others edged up as close as they could in the narrow tunnel.

'Is it the amulet?' breathed Jamie.

'I don't know,' said Tracy. She opened her fingers. The thing was a plate of dull brownish metal with a hole in each corner. 'There's something written on it.' She wiped her sleeve over the face of the metal oblong.

'What does it say?' asked Holly, stretching over Jamie's shoulder to try and see.

Tracy held it beside the light. 'It says . . . "Thomas Cropper, 1716 to 1754. Rest In Peace".' She gave a sudden scream and dropped the plate, shrinking away to the side of the tunnel.

'It's a coffin plate!' she wailed, her eyes round with horror. 'I've just put my hand into someone's grave!'

8 Where five strikes four

Belinda gave a horrified yell as the metal coffin plate dropped into her lap. She squirmed frantically in the confines of the tunnel, trying to dislodge the plate without touching it.

Tracy had balled herself up against the brick wall, her hands over her eyes, shuddering with revulsion.

Belinda gave a heave and the plate slid to the ground.

'Ow! Watch out!' shouted Jamie as Belinda's head came cracking back against his face. He sprawled backwards, tipping Holly over and landing on top of her.

The breath was forced out of Holly's lungs and she floundered in the damp earth like a stranded fish, flattened under Jamie's weight, and then squashed even further into the ground as Belinda came clambering over the two of them in her panic to get away from the ghastly metal plate.

The pandemonium lasted only a few chaotic seconds.

Belinda knelt, panting with shock, her panic subsiding now that Jamie and Holly were between her and the sheet of brown metal.

Holly shoved Jamie off her and sat up, her head reeling.

'For heaven's *sake*!' she gasped, her ears still ringing from Tracy's scream. 'Calm *down*, will you? Tracy!'

Tracy spread her fingers and looked down at the plate.

The thought of what she *might* have blindly got hold of through the hole in the wall made her blood run cold.

She took a few deep breaths, her eyes glued to the plate.

'I'm going back,' she said shakily. 'I've had it with this tunnel. I want out!'

Jamie sat up, his hand over his eye, his face throbbing with pain from the impact of the back of Belinda's head.

'I don't believe you lot,' he said, staring around at them with his one good eye. 'First, Holly smashes me in the nose with a door, then Belinda head-butts me in the eye.' He reached forward and picked up the plate, waving it in Tracy's face.

'It's just a bit of metal,' he said.

'Shut up!' cried Tracy. 'It's all right for you – you didn't put your hand into someone's grave.'

'Neither did you, I bet,' said Jamie. 'Who ever

113

heard of a grave with a brick wall round it? Talk sense!'

'He's right,' began Holly.

'What do you mean, he's right?' snapped Tracy. 'Look at it! What do you *think* it is? A greetings card? I'm telling you – that *thing* comes off a coffin.'

'Just a minute,' said Belinda. 'What exactly did you feel through the hole, Tracy?'

Tracy took a long breath. 'Nothing,' she said. 'Thank heavens, nothing *else*!'

'No earth?' asked Belinda.

'No. Nothing,' said Tracy. 'Look, you guys, can we chat about this later?'

'No, wait!' said Belinda. 'Jamie's right. Whatever there is behind that wall, it isn't a grave.'

'Thank you,' said Jamie. 'It's about time *someone* started listening to me.' He crawled forwards, lifting the lamp and holding it near the hole left by the missing brick. His injured eye was already beginning to close as he peered through the gap.

'Well?' said Holly, crawling up behind him.

'It's some kind of room,' said Jamie. 'I can't see much. Hold the lamp for me, Holly.'

'What are you doing?' Tracy asked.

'Making a bigger hole, if I can,' said Jamie. He jerked at the bricks round the hole. Damp mortar crumbled away as the bricks loosened. Jamie gave a shove with his shoulder and an entire section

114

of the wall swung outwards with a rumbling scrape.

He took the lamp from Holly and crawled through.

Holly looked at Tracy. 'Coming?' she said.

'No way,' said Tracy.

'If Jamie can do it, so can we,' said Belinda, coming up behind Holly. She grinned at Tracy. 'Last one through is a wet fish.' She stopped, turning her head to listen. She thought she had heard a faint sound from the depths of the tunnel.

'What is it?' asked Tracy.

'I'm not sure,' said Belinda. 'Blake, maybe? It can't have taken him long to find the tunnel. We haven't exactly been covering our tracks, have we? Come on, Tracy. This has got to be our way out of here.'

Holly stood up, glad at last to be able to stretch her aching back.

Jamie was standing holding the lamp aloft and staring around in silence. It was a strange room. It had a stone floor and a low, arched, stone roof supported on massive square pillars. Set into the aged brick walls were stone squares. The silence was absolute, making the throb of blood through Holly's temples sound as loud as drums.

'It's a crypt,' whispered Holly. She looked down. A small pile of coffin handles and plates lay on the

115

floor by the secret entrance. It was one of these plates that Tracy had caught hold of.

'Oh, lord!' breathed Belinda, gazing around. 'We must be under that church.' She walked along a wall, reading the carvings on the stones. 'They're all seventeen-hundred-and-something,' she said. 'This place can't have been used for ages.' A broad flight of stone steps led to a massive stone slab set into the ceiling. 'That's the way up into the church,' she said. 'It'll be sealed. But why does the tunnel lead here?'

Tracy straightened up, curious again now that she had recovered from her fright. 'Don't you remember what the vicar told us?' she said. 'When they went to the pub to arrest Oliver Duke, he wasn't there – even though they were certain he should have been. He must have escaped down the tunnel.'

'That's it!' said Holly. 'And they finally captured him in the waste land behind the church.' Her eyes widened. 'Now we know why. His escape tunnel led here. Which means there must be some way out.'

Belinda looked round at her. 'You mean there was *once*. Who knows if it still exists?'

'Look at this,' said Jamie. He had walked behind one of the pillars. Someone, who knows how long ago, had dug away into the brickwork of the wall, constructing a flight of uneven steps with the bricks that led up to a round hole. Jamie shone the lamp. The hole was capped by wooden boards.

'That's got to be the way out,' he said. His eyes gleamed. 'Just think!' he said. 'Oliver Duke must have done all this. Can you imagine it? Him prowling around here with a bag full of loot? Amazing!'

'Let's go for it,' said Tracy. 'I don't want to stay down here any longer than we have to. I've had just about enough of this.'

'Scared of ghosts?' grinned Jamie.

'No,' said Tracy. 'But I'm filthy and I'm freezing cold. I've had my fill of excitement for one day.'

Belinda crouched at the entrance to the tunnel. 'I can't hear anything,' she said. She shoved the brickwork entrance closed and fitted the loose brick back in place. 'That should slow Blake down a little, if he is still following us,' she said.

While Jamie held the lamp, Tracy climbed up into the hole in the wall and pushed against the boards.

'Any luck?' asked Holly.

'Yes,' said Tracy. 'I think so. It feels quite loose.' She pushed up hard and the boards lifted.

Holly watched as her friend's feet scrabbled at the edges of the rough-hewn hole. Tracy's legs vanished up into the hole and a few seconds later they heard her call down.

117

'Daylight!' she called. 'Come on, you guys, we're home free!'

One by one they clambered up the hole and came out into a narrow hallway. Slender arched windows showed a view filled with snow. While they had been underground, the weather had worsened considerably and the hallway was filled with an eerie grey snow-light.

At either side of the hall was a closed wooden door, arched like the windows.

'I was right,' said Belinda. 'We must be in the church.'

'"Above from below,"' quoted Holly. 'It's in the poem. Remember? "To where five strikes four, above from below."' She looked at her friends, her eyes shining. 'And the clock in the church tower struck eleven when it was really twelve o'clock. Don't you remember Belinda mentioning it? Oliver Duke must have meant the clock tower. It's the last bit of the poem.'

'I think we should go straight to the police and tell them about what that Blake guy has been up to,' said Tracy.

'But we're so close,' said Jamie. 'While we're looking for the police, he could have found the amulet and scarpered with it.'

'I don't care,' said Tracy. 'You do what you like – I'm out of here!' She walked determinedly to one of the doors and took hold of the black, iron loop that served as a handle. She looked over her shoulder. 'Anyone else with me?'

'She's right,' said Holly, looking at Jamie.

Tracy opened the door. It led directly to a flight of stairs winding upwards.

'That'll be the clock tower,' said Belinda. She opened the other door and they found themselves looking into the main part of the old church with its rows of dark wood pews and the altar standing beneath a soaring stained glass window.

'This is our way out,' she said. She frowned. 'But didn't the vicar tell us he keeps the place locked up?'

'There's bound to be *some* way out,' said Holly. 'Are you coming, Jamie?'

'No,' Jamie said vehemently. 'I'm going to have a look up in the tower.'

'Suit yourself,' said Tracy. 'You'll leave a nice trail up the stairs for Blake to follow.' They looked down. Their shoes were caked with mud from the tunnel.

'Oh, no I won't,' said Jamie. He knelt and took his shoes off. 'See? There won't be anything for him to follow now.'

'Jamie, please,' Holly coaxed. 'Don't be difficult.'

'I'm not being difficult,' said Jamie. His face brightened. 'In fact, if you three go off in the

119

other direction, Blake will probably follow the trail of mud you'll leave. That way, I can go up the tower without him knowing anything about it.' He grinned at them. 'That's it,' he said. 'You go off and get the police, if you like, while I find the amulet all by myself.'

The three girls looked at one another. By the look on Jamie's face, Holly could tell he was determined to have his own way. And arguing about it would only waste time. Not a good idea, if Blake really had followed them into the tunnel.

'I'll go with you,' said Holly with a sigh. She slipped her shoes off. 'He's right, I suppose,' she said, looking at Belinda and Tracy. 'Blake's likely to follow the muddy footprints, isn't he? You could lead him away from us while we go up the tower and see if there's anything up there.'

'I think you're mad,' said Tracy. 'Have you forgotten the rifle?'

'Huh!' exclaimed Jamie. 'I don't believe there ever was a rifle. You just imagined it – like you imagined you'd stuck your hand in a grave back there.'

'Let's do *something*, for heaven's sake,' said Belinda.

'Right,' agreed Holly. 'You and Tracy find a way out. Jamie and I will go up the tower.'

Jamie grinned. 'Brilliant!' he said. He stuck his tongue out at Tracy. She shook her head despairingly.

The staircase wound its way up the tall, square tower. Occasional narrow window slits let enough light in for Jamie and Holly to see their way as they padded up the bare treads with their shoes in their hands.

'I hope this is a good idea,' whispered Holly. She had a strong feeling that it might prove to be a very *bad* idea indeed. 'Your eye doesn't look very healthy. Does it hurt?'

'Only a bit,' said Jamie with a grin. 'Is it going black?'

'Not yet,' said Holly. 'But I'm sure it will. I don't know what Mum and Dad are going to say about it.'

'They won't mind – not when we tell them we've found treasure that's been hidden for two hundred years,' said Jamie.

'Don't be too sure about *that*,' said Holly. 'What gets me, is that I'm probably going to be blamed for getting you into all this. I always seem to be blamed when you get yourself into trouble.'

'The burden of being an older sister,' said Jamie with a grin. 'I feel so *sorry* for you.'

The steps ended in a lofty stone room in the centre of which hung a single huge bell in a wooden framework. To one side was the complex machinery of the clock, making gentle clicking sounds as the cogwheels turned. A spindle from the centre of the machine stretched out and pierced the stone wall.

Holly circled the bell and looked at the intricate workings of the clock.

'See anything?' asked Jamie.

'No,' said Holly. 'I don't even know where we should look.'

'The poem says: "where five strikes four",' said Jamie. 'It's got to be something to do with the clock.'

'But we can't *see* the clock from in here,' said Holly. She touched the metal spindle. 'Where five strikes four?' she said thoughtfully, looking at the wall.

'That's simple,' said Jamie, pointing. 'Twelve is up there – so four o'clock must be . . . here!' He described part of the circumference of a circle on the stones with his hand. 'There must be something here,' he said. 'Behind a stone. Come on, Holly – help me look.'

Holly shook her head. The wall showed no sign of having been tampered with, and the stones were too large for anyone to have shifted them.

Jamie crouched by the wall, trying to spot some way of moving any of the stones. He took out his keys and scraped at the mortar that held the stones together.

As Holly watched, a small chunk of mortar fell away from under one of the stones.

Jamie let out a soft whistle, digging deeper into the wall with the point of his key. 'Holly!' he breathed. 'I think this is it! Really! Look!'

Holly knelt beside him. His key had scratched out a small hole in the wall.

'There's something in there,' she said. Jamie's key chinked against a coin-sized disc of dark brown metal. 'Can you get it out?'

Jamie worked at the mortar around the metal disk.

'We've found it, Holly,' he breathed. 'I *knew* we would.' he looked round at her. 'You never really believed me, did you?'

She smiled. 'No, not really,' she said. 'But let's find out what it is first. Can you pull it out yet?'

'I think so,' said Jamie. He wormed his fingers into the hole. The thing he pulled out was a narrow copper tube made of two halves that slid together.

Jamie frowned. 'Is this what an amulet looks like?' he said.

'I wouldn't have thought so,' said Holly. 'Can you get it open?'

Jamie tugged at the two ends of the tube. 'It's stuck,' he said.

'Give it here,' said Holly. The tube was about ten centimetres long. She twisted the two ends in opposite directions and it broke apart. Curled in the hollow of the tube was a small twist of paper.

Very gently, Holly took the paper out. It was yellowed with age and felt brittle in her fingers.

'Open it, then,' urged Jamie.

'Wait,' said Holly. 'We've got to be careful. It looks like it might fall to pieces if we're too rough with it.'

She rested the curl of paper on the floor and cautiously unfurled it.

There were four lines of writing on it, in ink that had faded over the years to the palest of browns:

> *In heart of oak it is buried deep.*
> *And below the hungry worms will creep.*
> *If thou should'st seek, good luck to thee,*
> *For my luck dies on the gallows tree.*

'What does it mean?' asked Jamie.

Holly shook her head. 'It means the amulet is somewhere else,' she said. 'It's just another clue.'

'But it means we're on the right trail,' said Jamie. 'And we're getting closer.'

'I suppose so,' said Holly. She smiled at Jamie. 'Now we've got to try and get out of here without bumping into Blake.' Her face brightened. 'Don't you see? We've got the next clue. The poem just leads here. If we take this away with us, he won't know what to do next.' She stood up, a new energy flowing through her. 'Come on,' she said. 'Let's find Tracy and Belinda – and then let's get out of here.'

'To find the amulet?' said Jamie.

'No,' said Holly. 'To get the police.'

She led the way back down the twisting staircase.

'Couldn't we look for the amulet first?' whispered Jamie.

'No,' said Holly. 'I've had enough of being chased by Tony Blake. We've got to do something about him. If there really is an amulet, it won't be going anywhere, will it? Besides which, we're going to give this clue to that Tessa woman you eavesdropped on. She'll be arriving here this afternoon, if you remember. If anyone deserves to find the amulet, it's *her*, not us.'

'After all the trouble we've been to?' said Jamie. 'You're just going to hand it all over to someone else?'

'Yes,' said Holly. 'That's exactly what I'm going to do.'

The door to the hallway had swung shut.

Holly put her finger to her lips. 'Keep absolutely quiet,' she whispered. 'Blake might already be in here, for all we know.'

She turned the heavy iron handle and pulled the door open.

Her heart leaped into her throat at the sight that greeted her.

'Don't move,' said Tony Blake. 'I knew you'd be nearby.' A grimace twisted his mouth. 'Get in here.'

Holly stared in shock into the hallway. Tracy and Belinda were standing silently against one wall, their eyes filled with despair.

Tony Blake held a hunting rifle, pointing it towards them. He swung the muzzle of the rifle to face Holly and Jamie.

'Do as I say,' he ordered. 'Do exactly as I tell you, or someone will get hurt.'

9 Lost in the blizzard

Holly stared at the rifle, her hand groping automatically backwards, her fingers closing protectively on Jamie's arm.

'Move over next to your friends,' said Tony Blake, jerking the rifle sideways.

Following them through the tunnel had left its marks on the man. His coat and hands were grimy with earth; sweat trickled down his pudgy red face. The hands that held the rifle were trembling.

'I won't tell you again,' he said.

Tracy eyed the rifle. In a film, this would be the moment – while his attention was distracted – to take a flying leap at him, disarm him and wrestle him to the ground. Except that they weren't in a film, and Tony Blake looked nervous enough to let fly with the rifle at the slightest movement.

The vicar had been telling the truth about the church. Tracy and Belinda had found the main doors locked shut. They had been creeping along towards the back, hoping to find another way out, when Tony Blake had caught them.

They had tried to convince him that Holly and Jamie were gone – gone for the police. But he hadn't believed them.

Their only hope had been that Holly would see their predicament and be able to escape without being seen herself. That hope had been dashed at the opening of the clock tower door.

'There's no need for guns,' said Holly, noticing the way Tony Blake's eyes were shifting uneasily behind his spectacles. 'We won't do anything.'

'Was it there?' asked Blake, his eyes searching over them. 'Have you found it?'

'Is it really so important?' murmured Belinda. 'Is it really worth all *this*?'

His eyes flickered towards her. 'I want that amulet,' he said. 'I know what it's worth, even if you don't.'

'Worth going to prison for?' said Tracy.

Blake's eyes narrowed and his mouth spread in a mirthless grin. 'Worth *avoiding* prison for,' he said.

Holly took a deep breath, swallowing hard. 'Please put that gun down,' she said. 'What harm can we do you?'

Blake's brows knitted. 'Did you *find* it?' he asked angrily.

'There was nothing there,' said Jamie. 'Go and look for yourself if you don't believe us.'

128

'Did you search?' There was a tremor of frustration in Tony Blake's voice. 'Did you search properly?'

'We searched everywhere,' said Holly. 'There's nothing there.'

Tony Blake wiped a grubby sleeve over his forehead. 'It must be,' he hissed. 'It *must* be there. No one can have found it. Not after all this time.'

'If you put that rifle down,' said Belinda gently, 'we'll help you look for it.'

For a moment it almost seemed that he might lower the gun. Holly could see the conflict of emotions chasing across his sweating face.

'Why are you doing this?' she asked coaxingly. If she could only get him talking, perhaps he really would put the gun down. 'Do you know something about the amulet?'

Tony Blake licked his lips. 'I know that it's more valuable than you could possibly realise,' he stammered. 'I know that if I find it, I'll be able to . . .' His voice trailed off, as if he suddenly realised that he was saying more than he had intended.

'Did you know about the amulet before you overheard us talking about it?' asked Holly. *Keep him talking*, she thought. *Keep him talking and he'll calm down. Then we'll be safe.*

'I'd heard the stories,' said Tony Blake. 'I was born in this village. Everyone here knows about Oliver Duke.'

'He's some kind of local legend, huh?' asked Tracy, noticing how Tony Blake's grip on the rifle was gradually loosening. 'Like Robin Hood?'

Tony Blake swung the rifle towards her. 'Shut up,' he said. 'Do you think I'm stupid? Do you? Do you think you can keep me talking here until someone comes along to rescue you?'

'No,' said Tracy. 'I'm sorry.'

'The amulet isn't up there,' shouted Jamie.

Tony Blake turned to stare at him. 'Why are you so certain?' he said. 'You didn't have time to search everywhere.'

'We didn't need to,' blurted Jamie. 'Let us go.'

Tony Blake moved towards him, the gun level again. 'Not until you tell me why you're so sure it's not there,' he said. His eyes narrowed dangerously. 'What *did* you find?' he asked.

'I'm not telling you!' shouted Jamie. 'You stole my book, and you locked me up. I'm not telling you *anything*!'

'Oh, yes, you will,' Blake snarled angrily.

Holly realised that it was too late now to pretend there hadn't been anything up in the tower. Jamie's outburst had made it obvious that they had discovered something.

'Here.' She took the metal tube out of her pocket. She had slipped the roll of old paper back into it for safe-keeping. 'We found this.'

'Holly!' exclaimed Jamie.

She glanced round at him. 'It's no good,' she said. 'It's too dangerous to lie any more.'

'Give it to me,' said Blake.

He let go of the rifle with one hand, reaching out to take the tube from Holly.

'Don't!' screamed Tracy. For a single moment, Tony Blake's attention was distracted by the sudden noise. Holly lashed her arm out sideways, hitting the muzzle of the rifle, almost wrenching it clean out of his hand.

Before he could recover, she hurled herself forwards, crashing into his chest with her shoulder, sending him stumbling backwards.

His heels caught on the loosened boards that lay at the side of the hole that led up from the crypt. His arms windmilled as he lost balance.

'Quick!' yelled Tracy, wrenching open the door that led into the church.

Holly pounced forwards as Blake came crashing down onto his back. Jamie was only an instant behind her.

The four of them hurtled through the doorway. Tony Blake sprawled on his back, his breath coming out in a shout of rage.

Tracy slammed the door closed on him.

'Lock it!' yelled Belinda.

'I can't!' gasped Tracy, clinging to the black handle. 'There's nothing to lock it *with*!'

'You should have grabbed the rifle!' shouted Belinda.

'I got us out of there, didn't I?' gasped Holly. 'I can't think of everything.' She stared round the church. 'Is there a way out?'

'Not the front way,' said Belinda.

'The back!' shouted Tracy. 'Try the back!'

They went skidding through the rows of pews, heading helter-skelter towards the rear of the church. In the darkened corner beyond the pulpit they could see a door.

'Stop!' Tony Blake's voice echoed through the church.

Tracy cannoned against the door, wrenching the handle and almost falling as the door flew open.

The others piled in behind her and she slammed the door shut, seeing for an instant through the crack that Tony Blake was running through the pews towards them. And he still had the rifle.

They were in a small ante-room. There was a table, a few chairs and a row of dark wood cupboards. But that was not all. To their relief, they saw another door. A door that led to the outside.

'Get the table!' said Holly.

The four of them dragged the heavy table across to block the door through which they had just come.

That should give us a few moments, Holly thought hopefully.

The outer door was bolted at the top and bottom. Belinda and Tracy heaved at the bolts, yanking them back and pulling the door open.

A blast of freezing, snow-filled air gushed in over them. The snow was already beginning to settle, dappling the grass with a lacework of white.

They heard the crash of Tony Blake hitting against the other door. There was no time to think. The door was already a few inches open and the table was being pushed inwards by the force of Tony Blake's attack.

'Run!' shouted Holly.

They ploughed out into the whipping blizzard, their eyes filled with snow. Jamie ran forward, heading for the low wall that surrounded the churchyard.

'No!' shouted Holly. 'Jamie! Not that way!'

But Jamie was too scared to pay any attention to his sister's frantic shout. The only thought in his mind was to get away.

'You're running the wrong way!' yelled Tracy. 'Jamie! The *other* way! Back to the village!'

'I'll get him,' shouted Holly against the whip of the swirling wind.

Belinda stumbled in Jamie's wake, her glasses covered with snow.

Holly overtook her, but Jamie was already through the gate in the wall and running full tilt across the open ground towards the trees.

133

The two girls slithered on the wet grass as they tried to get through the gateway.

Jamie, his heels kicking up snow, was almost in the trees. They redoubled their efforts, feet sliding as they chased after him. They reached the trees. Here, the ground was bare and dry and the full force of the blizzard reduced to a splintered howling that rattled the naked branches above their heads.

'Jamie!' shouted Holly, raking her eyes across the panorama of black tree trunks.

'There!' gasped Belinda, pointing. She had seen a brief glimpse of Jamie's coat through the trees.

The two girls ran after him. Here and there fallen trees blocked their way. They fought through dense, snagging sprays of bare undergrowth.

Holly came to a panting halt. 'Where *is* he?' she gasped, a stitch knifing into her side. 'Where's he *gone*?'

'Holly! Here!' Holly snapped her head round. She saw Jamie beckon to her from behind the earth-clogged roots of a fallen tree.

'You idiot!' she shouted. 'It's all open countryside this way!'

Jamie's head and shoulders appeared over the thick trunk. 'Is he after us?' he called.

The two girls ran round the fallen tree. Belinda slumped to the ground, panting heavily, her back to the tree trunk. Holly ducked, looking back the way they had come. Snow knifed its way through the trees, but there was no sign of any other movement.

'Why did you come this way?' groaned Belinda. 'The village is in the opposite direction. Blake's between us and the *village*, now!'

'It's not my fault,' said Jamie. 'Holly said run. So I ran.' He looked anxiously at his sister. 'Can you see him?'

'No,' said Holly. 'Not yet. It'll only be a matter of time, though. Oh, *Jamie*, how could you be so stupid?'

'I'm not—' Jamie's protest was cut dead by a sudden noise. A sharp, echoey crack, sounding clearly above the whirl of the wind.

'What was that?' whispered Holly. 'Did you hear it?'

Belinda turned onto her knees and lifted her head above the ridge of the trunk. 'It was a shot,' she said. She stared at Holly. 'It was a rifle shot.'

The same terrible thought struck both of them at the same moment.

'Tracy!' gasped Holly. 'Where's Tracy?'

'I don't know,' said Belinda. 'Did you see which way she went?'

'No,' said Holly. 'You don't . . . you don't think he *got* her?'

'She'd have been too quick for him,' said Belinda. 'You know how fast she can run.' She looked uneasily at Holly. 'He can't have *shot* her. He can't. You saw how nervous he was with that gun. I can't believe he'd really shoot anyone.'

'I've got to go back,' said Holly, standing up. 'She could be hurt.'

'I'll come with you,' said Belinda.

'No,' Holly said fiercely. '*I'll* go. We can't risk all of us getting caught. You and Jamie can try circling round and getting back to the village. That way at least *someone* will be able to get help.'

'OK,' said Belinda. 'And don't worry.' She gave Holly a reassuring smile. 'Chances are Tracy's already got to the village.'

Holly looked down at her. 'So what was Blake shooting at?' she said grimly.

She didn't wait for an answer.

She ran back the way they had come. It took longer to find the edge of the wood than she had expected. Something about the shriek of the wind and the constant battering of sharp snow crystals in her eyes disorientated her.

She gave a gasp of relief as she glimpsed open ground. The dark, snow-swept shape of the church was away over to her left. Even in that short space of time, she had wandered off course. Although there was no sign of Blake, it took all her courage for Holly to come out of the trees and run, crouching, towards the church.

She knelt behind the low wall, trying to control

her breathing as she gradually lifted her head over the parapet.

Out of the corner of her eye she saw a grey figure running through the curtains of snow. Too big and slow to be Tracy, it ran away to her right, outside the circle of the churchyard wall, heading away from the village.

Tony Blake! thought Holly. There was no mistaking him, and even with her eyes full of snow, she could see the dark shape of the rifle in his hands. He was running fast. Chasing someone that Holly couldn't see. But she didn't need to see to know that he had to be chasing Tracy.

A wave of relief swept over Holly. She had half-dreaded to see Tracy lying shot in the snow. But Tracy might still be hurt. Running, but injured by Blake's bullet.

Holly went through an agony of indecision. The way was clear for her to escape now to the village – but that would mean abandoning Tracy. No, she couldn't do that. Jamie and Belinda would raise the alarm. Her duty was to try and find some way of helping Tracy. She couldn't do anything else.

She ran, bent over, along the line of the wall, using it as cover until she came to the corner.

Tony Blake was ahead of her, his coat trailing out behind him as he pounded along towards the trees that formed a half-circle around the back of the churchyard.

If she could get into the trees unseen, maybe she could outdistance him and find Tracy. She hesitated for a few moments in the lee of the wall, watching the ghostly shape of Tony Blake disappear into the trees. Then she ran, her heart hammering as she swerved away from the place where she had seen him push into the woods, her mind filled with the desperate hope that she would be able to find Tracy before he did.

'Which way now?' asked Jamie, looking at Belinda.

The two of them had followed Holly's plan, or at least they had *tried* to.

They had set off into the woods, intending to make their way parallel to the open ground behind the churchyard for a distance, and then to change course towards the village.

But the woods had proved more confusing than they had anticipated.

Belinda stared round into the baffling woodland.

'I don't know,' she said. 'We should have hit open land by now.' She punched in futility at a tree trunk. 'This stupid wood!' she exclaimed. 'It all looks the same.' She rubbed her hand. 'I can't tell which way to go,' she said.

'This way,' said Jamie, setting off in exactly the opposite direction to the one Belinda would have chosen.

She shook her head, plodding along behind him, huddled in her coat against the teeming snow. The wood couldn't go on for ever, she thought. They were bound to hit a road or something soon.

'I was right!' said Jamie.

Belinda lifted her eyes. There was a break in the endless crowding of trees, only a little way ahead.

'Jamie, you're brilliant!' said Belinda.

They ran forward, relieved beyond words to be finally out of the meandering woods.

There was only one problem. A tall, wire fence stretched across their exit, stretching a good two metres into the air. The ground sloped suddenly ahead of them beyond the fence and they found themselves looking down into a shallow cutting with railway lines running along it.

Beyond the cutting there was snowswept countryside with not a building in sight.

Jamie climbed the fence and dropped to the ground on the far side.

'Come on,' he said, looking back at Belinda. 'All we've got to do is follow the railway.

Belinda eyed the fence uneasily. Jamie had gone up and over it like a monkey, making it look easy.

She gripped the rusty wire and lifted a foot, pushing the toe of her shoe into one of the diamond-shaped holes. She lifted herself clear of the ground.

The fence swayed and bounced under her

weight, taking her by surprise. Her foot slipped out and she fell on to her knees with a yell.

It did nothing for her self-esteem to see the contemptuous expression on Jamie's face as he looked at her through the fence.

'Don't say a word,' she puffed, getting to her feet. 'I slipped, that's all.'

'Try climbing nearer one of the posts,' suggested Jamie. 'It won't wobble around so much.'

'I was just about to,' said Belinda. 'I don't need your advice.'

'No,' murmured Jamie under his breath. 'What you need is a crane.'

'I heard that,' said Belinda. 'Don't you be so cheeky, Jamie Adams.' Fired with a new determination to prove to Jamie that she wasn't entirely useless, Belinda moved along the fence to one of the iron posts. She stretched up and caught hold of the top of the fence. It swayed a little as she scrabbled for a foothold.

She heaved herself upwards. Her head came up above the fence. She pushed down on the post and managed to get her top half onto the shaking lip of zigzagging wire. She stretched a leg, trying to hook her foot over the top. The head of the post thrust painfully into her stomach.

'Take your time,' said Jamie. 'I mean, we're not in any particular hurry, are we?'

'Jamie,' panted Belinda. 'Do you want another black eye?'

'No, thanks, one's enough,' said Jamie.

'Shut up, then,' groaned Belinda.

She got her foot over the top and let her centre of balance shift over the fence. She wavered for a few painful moments then tried to let herself down on the other side.

She gave a strangled croak. Her coat had caught on something. She half-fell, her coat tangling up around her neck. She came to a sudden halt, caught fast on the fence, her coat wrapped around her like a straightjacket, her legs waving helplessly in the air.

Jamie spluttered with laughter, but then he stopped, his head turning.

'Jamie,' choked Belinda. 'Help me.'

'There's a train coming,' said Jamie. 'We can flag it down.'

'No, Jamie, don't!' shouted Belinda. 'It's not safe!'

But Jamie ignored her. He slithered down the bank and scrambled towards the tracks.

'Jamie!' yelled Belinda, hearing the rush of the oncoming train roaring above the wailing of the snowfilled wind. She struggled to free herself, but only succeeded in getting herself more firmly entangled.

Helplessly she watched as Jamie ran down

towards the railway tracks, his arms waving in the air as the speeding train burst into view.

She saw him slip and fall.

'Jamie!' she screamed, her voice drowned out by the roar of the train. 'Jamie!'

10 Hunted!

It took all of Tracy's agility and concentration to keep on her feet as she bounded through the trees. Icy air tore her throat and she screwed her eyes up against the spinning snow. The ground was uneven and she had to twist and turn to avoid the looming trees.

She had hesitated at the church door, seeing Holly and Belinda running off into the thick wall of snow in pursuit of Jamie. She knew she could have easily outdistanced them, but that would have sent them all in the wrong direction. She didn't know the area at all. She had no idea where the trees led. All she *did* know was that Jamie and the two girls were running *away* from the village, and that their only hope of salvation lay in the *opposite* direction.

She had to get somewhere where there were people. Any people. The railway station! That was it. If she could get to the railway station, someone would help them.

From within the church she heard the crash of

the table that they had used to block the inner door falling over. Tony Blake was only seconds behind them. Tracy spun round, grasping the handle of the outer door and jerking the door shut.

She felt pressure on the handle from within. Strong hands had taken hold of it and there was nothing she could do to stop the slow, relentless turning. Desperation lent her strength. She applied all her weight and the handle turned back to the locked position.

But the snow made it slippery. She felt the handle skidding through her fingers. She jammed her heels up hard aginst the doorstep and heaved backwards as the door edged a crack open. The muscles in her shoulders twisted with the effort. It felt as if her arms were being yanked out of their sockets.

Strong as she was, there was no way she could prevail for long against the power of a grown man hauling at the door from the other side.

She was losing the uneven tug-of-war. The door was a couple of centimetres open now. Another second or two and Blake would tear the door wide open and she'd be facing that rifle again.

Her feet slid on the doorstep. She felt her grip sliding on the wet handle. She gave a yell of alarm as the handle finally slithered out of her hands and she fell over backwards on to the path.

The door flew open and she heard a crash,

followed by the piercingly loud *crack*! of the rifle going off.

She scrambled to her feet, taking an instant to look through the open doorway before she fled. Tony Blake was in a heap on the floor, the rifle fallen to one side, his eyes wide with shock.

Tracy almost felt like laughing. Of course! She realised what had happened. Blake had been exerting as much pressure to get the door open as she had been to keep it closed. The sudden lack of force caused by Tracy losing her grip on the handle had sent him tumbling over backwards. The falling rifle had gone off on its own.

Tracy darted alongside the church wall. But Blake was on his feet and out into the blizzard in a second.

Get into cover! thought Tracy. *Quickly*! It was all open ground between here and the railway. There was nowhere to hide. She didn't *think* Blake would shoot at her, but she couldn't be sure. She had no time to debate with herself about *what* he might be capable of.

The low churchyard wall stretched between her and a shielding barrier of trees. If she could get into those trees, maybe she could lose Blake.

She vaulted the wall and headed at breakneck speed for the trees. She risked a glance round. Blake, the rifle in one hand, was clambering awkwardly over the wall.

A glow of hope ignited within her. He was slow and heavy. She could outrun him.

Her hair plastered wetly over her face as she zigzagged through the woods.

She flung another look over her shoulder. She couldn't see him, nor could she hear any sounds of pursuit above the wail of the wind. Not that *that* meant much. She wanted to be sure of a good lead on him before she dared to slow down.

She took deep, measured breaths, trying to ignore the way the air froze her lungs.

At last she slowed to a jog, straining her ears for any sound above the wind.

She grinned. She had deliberately run an erratic course through the woodland, planning on him losing all trace of her. The only problem now was that she had little idea of where she was herself.

The village is to my left, she said to herself, altering course and jogging steadily in that direction. *No problem, Tracy. No problem at all.*

She hit on a break in the trees. A broad swathe cut through the woods.

'The railway!' she panted, seeing the tracks running across her path. But there was something wrong. Instead of the usual bright gleam of steel, the tracks were brown and rusted, with weeds growing among the sleepers.

She stepped out into the open. Her wild flight had not given her time to notice it, but now she was still, she could see that the wind had eased off. The snow still teemed thickly down, but the whipping wind had abated. The spiteful razor-edge of the blizzard had passed.

This isn't the real railway, thought Tracy. *This is just some abandoned old siding or something*.

All the same, surely it had to lead back to the main line. And once she hit the railway, it would take her only a little while to follow it back to the village.

She began to jog alongside the tracks, praying that Tony Blake had gone in some other direction.

Something large and dark loomed out of the snow. At first, her eyes befuddled by the thick flakes that swarmed all around her, Tracy thought it was a building. But as she got closer she saw that it was a railway wagon.

A freight wagon standing alone on the disused line. Left there for some reason, its wheels as rusty as the tracks on which it stood. Tracy looked up at its tall sides. Its door was open and she could see crates and empty sacks lying inside.

She was about to pass by the wagon when she heard a noise from in amongst the trees. The sharp crack of a twig breaking. Her senses immediately became alert. Now that the wind had died down, every sound seemed to be amplified in the eerie snow-heavy silence – everything from the crunch of her own feet on the weed-infested gravel, to the rasp of her breath.

She heard more movements. In all this snow, Blake could be only a few metres away and she might not be able to see him. But the sounds she heard were definitely those of someone moving through the trees.

Tracy grinned as an idea came to her. Rather than making a run for it, perhaps this wagon could give her the chance of actually *capturing* Blake. She clambered up into the wagon. The broad door on the far side was shut. She knew how these doors worked. They were opened and shut by a lever on the outside of the wagon. Once shut, there was no way of getting them open from inside.

She looked up. There were a couple of hatches in the roof. Air vents. Small square-lidded openings. Working fast, she dragged a crate under one of the vents and climbed on to it. She reached up and pushed at the lid of the vent. It was loose. The gap was too narrow for someone the size of Tony Blake to get through, but she would be able to manage it.

She jumped down and edged an eye around the open doorway. Blake was still not in sight and she couldn't hear anything. She had to draw his attention to the wagon. Make it obvious that she was in there. That way, with any luck, he would follow her in.

She edged out of sight, her heart hammering in her chest.

Now or never, she thought. She clasped her hands together. 'Please let it work,' she whispered.

She gave one of the empty crates a hefty kick. There was a loud clatter as the crate fell over. Surely Blake couldn't have failed to have heard that?

A nervous smile crept over her face as she heard a noise from outside the wagon. It had worked! She heard him come crunching across the gravel.

But she had to be quick. She jumped up on to the crate she had positioned beneath the vent and stretched her arms up. As she strained her muscles to pull herself up, she heard the sound of Blake climbing up to the high open doorway of the wagon.

She pulled herself out on to the roof and slid the lid of the vent back in place. As silently as possible, she crawled to the edge of the curved roof. He was inside! She couldn't see him, but she could hear him in there.

She trailed a leg over the side of the wagon, shoving her heel up hard against the top edge of the sliding door. For a second she was afraid it wouldn't move. But then, with a terrific grinding of rusty metal, it grated sideways and closed with an echoing boom.

It was quite a jump down to ground level. Tracy

bent her legs as she launched herself off the roof. She landed well. A second later she had jumped up and caught hold of the locking lever. It crashed into place.

She had done it! She let out a yell of triumph, almost dancing with delight.

'Got you!' she shouted, beating a tattoo on the locked door with both hands. 'You've had it, mister! That'll teach you to mess with us!'

A sudden sound behind her made her spin round.

She gave a gasp of horror. Tony Blake stood at the edge of the trees, his eyes burning into her, the rifle levelled towards her.

'What the . . .' Her voice faded as Tony Blake stepped out from under the trees. There was a frantic hammering from inside the wagon.

'Tracy!' It was Holly's voice. 'Tracy! it's *me*! Let me out of here.'

Tracy's legs almost collapsed under her with shock. Her brilliant trap had worked perfectly. There was only one problem. She had trapped the wrong person.

'You'd better let her out,' said Blake, motioning towards her with the rifle. 'Come on, get moving. I've run out of patience with you kids.'

Her heart sinking down to her shoes, Tracy climbed the side of the wagon and released the locking lever. The heavy door slid open.

'Tracy! You maniac! What on earth are you – *oh*!'
Holly looked down at Blake. 'Oh! *Tracy*!'

'Get down out of there,' said Tony Blake. 'And if either of you tries *anything*, I'll use this.' He nodded towards the rifle.

Holly let herself down out of the wagon and the two girls stood waiting to see what Tony Blake would do next.

He stared at Holly. 'I'll have that thing you found in the clock tower now,' he said. 'You've got three seconds to hand it over.'

'There's no need for threats,' said Holly. She felt in her coat pocket and drew the metal tube out. 'Here,' she said. 'Take it. It's just another rhyme.'

'Throw it to me,' said Blake.

She tossed it and he caught it, keeping the rifle tucked under one arm, his finger on the trigger. He was too wary to let them near enough to do anything.

He fumbled the tube open and unfurled the roll of paper with the fingers of one hand, his eyes constantly darting from them to the paper.

'Damn!' he said, his eyes narrowing as he read the brief clue. 'So he didn't hide it in the church.' A cold smile widened his mouth. '"In heart of oak it is buried deep",' he said. His eyes gleamed as he looked up at them. 'In heart of oak.' He let out a brief laugh. 'The oak tree! Oliver Duke asked to be buried under the oak tree at the

151

back of the church. Of *course*! *That* was where he hid it.'

Holly and Tracy looked at each other. Holly hadn't been given a moment to think about the meaning of the clue, but she felt sure that Tony Blake must have guessed right. Realising that capture was imminent, Oliver Duke must have fled along his secret tunnel. He must originally have hidden the amulet in the tower, like in the poem in the book, but he had *moved* it. Probably hoping that, even if he was captured, his daughter would be able to follow the second poem and find the amulet.

But then Oliver Duke had been caught and his daughter had left the village. She couldn't ever have found the second poem. It had lain hidden between the stones of the old clock tower for two hundred years.

'OK, you two,' said Blake. 'I think it's time we went and found the amulet.' He motioned them forward with the rifle. 'And if either of you gives me any trouble . . .' He didn't need to finish the threat.

The two girls walked ahead of him through the snow, only too well aware of the rifle trained at their backs.

The thunderous roar of the train shook the ground as Belinda struggled to get herself free of the fence. There was no sign of Jamie.

She could only pray that he had fallen at the side of the track and not under the wheels of the train.

There was a ripping noise and Belinda fell. Tangled up in her coat, she rolled down the embankment, only half-aware of the diminishing noise as the train sped away. Her vision was an alternating pattern of grass and sky as she rolled.

She hit something and came to a breathless halt. Her head spinning, she heard a groan from underneath her. Floundering in her torn coat, she sat up. Miraculously her spectacles had stayed in place.

Jamie writhed underneath her.

'I thought the train had hit me,' he groaned.

'I thought the train had hit you, you nutcase,' spluttered Belinda. 'I thought you'd run straight under it.'

'I slipped,' said Jamie. 'You're sitting on my legs.'

'Sorry,' said Belinda. 'Are you hurt?'

Jamie gave a hollow laugh. 'Am I hurt?' he said. 'Of course I'm hurt. You'd be hurt if a two-ton rhinoceros had just landed on you. I'm flat as a kipper!'

'One more crack about my weight,' warned Belinda, clambering giddily to her feet, 'and you'll be sucking your food through a straw. I'll . . .' The surrounding treetops did a hectic dance in front of her eyes. '*Ooh!*' she gasped. 'My *head!*'

Jamie stood up, feeling all over himself for damage. 'At least you got over the fence,' he said. 'I thought you'd be hanging there like a scarecrow all day.'

Belinda examined her coat. There was a big tear down the back. 'I never come out of any of Holly's mad schemes without *something* in tatters,' she said. 'I ought to start charging her for repairs.'

'And I'll send you my hospital bills,' said Jamie. 'Shall we go?'

'Oh, heavens, *yes*!' said Belinda. 'Anything could be happening back there. We must have wasted so much time.'

'And whose fault is that?' said Jamie.

Belinda gave him a deadly glare.

He looked up into the sky. 'At least the wind's died down a bit,' he said, wiping snowflakes out of his eyes. He trudged away along the railway line. 'Come on,' he said.

She ran to catch up with him.

'What did you and Holly actually find in the clock tower?' she asked.

As they walked along, Jamie explained about the metal container. He recited the rhyme to her.

'I haven't the foggiest idea what he was on about, though,' said Jamie. 'He was a total loony, if you ask me.'

'I don't think so,' Belinda said thoughtfully. She looked round at him. 'Of course,' she said. 'You weren't there when the vicar told us about the oak tree, were you?'

154

'What oak tree?'

'Oliver Duke asked to be buried under a particular oak tree. At the back of the church,' explained Belinda. 'That's what the rhyme must refer to. "In heart of oak" must mean he hid the amulet in *that* tree.'

They rounded a broad bend in the tracks.

Jamie let out a shout and began to run. Ahead of them through the snow they could see the roofs of houses. Only a hundred metres away Belinda saw the platform of the station.

She ran after him. At last, they would be able to get help for Holly and Tracy!

There was no sign of the train. Judging by the speed it had been doing, Belinda assumed it must have been an express. They ran up the platform slope.

A man in a railway uniform appeared, his face thunderous.

'Were you trespassing on the track?' he stormed before they had the chance to say anything. 'Have you got any idea how dangerous that is? It's a good job the police are here already. It'll save me having to call them.'

'The police?' shouted Belinda. 'Are they here? Get them. Quickly. Our friends are in danger.'

'Who wants the police?' A policeman came out of the station building. 'What's going on?'

'These two were trespassing on the line,' said

155

the man in the railway uniform. 'I think you'd
better—'

'Will you *listen*!' shouted Belinda. 'There's a crazy
man with a rifle out there.' She waved an arm
towards the church. 'You've got to *do* something!'

The policeman frowned at her. 'What man? What
is all this?'

Belinda nearly screamed with frustration. It was
maddening the way adults could be so *thick*!

'His name is Tony Blake,' Jamie broke in. 'He's
after the amulet! He's got a rifle. You've got to
get him. He's out there with my sister, *right
now*!'

The expression on the policeman's face changed.
'What name did you say?'

'Tony Blake!' Belinda yelled. 'What does it matter? He's going to *kill* them, you buffoon!'

The policeman stared for a moment, as if he
was considering how to respond to being called
a buffoon.

'Come with me,' he said. 'I've heard that name
recently.'

He ran through the station building, Jamie and
Belinda hot on his heels.

A police car was parked on the tarmac outside
the station.

'Frank,' called the policeman. Another officer
climbed out of the car. 'We've got a lead on
that Blake case,' he said. 'These two say they've

156

seen him.' He looked round at Belinda. 'How far?' he asked.

'Not far,' panted Belinda. 'Near the church.' She had no idea why they should already know Tony Blake's name. All that she was concerned with was that they should get after him – before something terrible happened out there.

'Apparently he's armed,' said the first policeman to his companion. 'Phone for assistance. I'll go with these two.'

'At last!' gasped Belinda. 'This way!'

She ran towards the church, Jamie and the policeman running alongside her.

She only hoped that they weren't already too late.

11 Peril on the tracks

The snow was starting to settle now that it was no longer being whipped up by the wind. Holly and Tracy's coats were blanketed with it as they stumbled through the trees, and their hair dripped icy water into their eyes.

Holly looked round. Tony Blake's glasses were frosted with ice crystals and his thin hair hung lank over his forehead. His cheeks burned red with the effort of tripping and sliding over hidden obstacles.

He looked like he was at the end of his tether, thought Holly. Hardly surprising, considering the exertions they had put him through in the past few hours. He didn't give the impression of being particularly fit.

'Stop!' he said.

The two girls halted and turned to look at him. Crooking the rifle under one arm, he wiped at his glasses with wet, stubby fingers. He looked anxiously around. Bare, black trees marched to the edge of sight in all directions.

'Kind of confusing, isn't it?' offered Tracy.

He stared at her. 'What?'

She spread her arms, indicating the trackless wood. 'All this,' she said. 'I guess it must be kind of difficult to know where you're going. Maybe you should have kept to the railway?'

'When I want your opinion, I'll ask for it,' he snapped.

'I was only trying to be helpful,' Tracy said mildly. 'But I guess you know where you're going?'

'You've got a smart mouth, girl,' said Blake. 'Keep it shut.'

'Oh, come on,' said Tracy. 'Admit it. You're lost.'

'Tracy!' warned Holly as the rifle rose in his hands.

'No,' said Tracy, turning square on to Tony Blake. 'I'm sick of this.' She glared at him. 'Look here, mister, I don't know what the big deal is with you and this amulet, but I *do* know a couple of things. Firstly, you don't have a clue where we're headed; and second, there's no way you're going to use that gun on us.'

'I will if you carry on provoking me,' said Blake.

'Oh, *sure* you will,' said Tracy. 'You're some big, bad bandit, you are! I bet you leave a trail of corpses every which way you go, huh?'

Holly wasn't sure what Tracy thought she was doing, but provoking Tony Blake seemed like a

159

dangerous game. All Holly wanted was to get this business over without anything terrible happening.

'Shut up!' Blake's shout was startlingly loud. He raised the rifle and pointed it straight at Tracy. 'One more word out of you . . .'

Holly darted in front of Tracy, her hands spread out towards Tony Blake.

'Calm down,' she said. 'Please, just calm down. She doesn't mean anything.'

The rifle was lowered. 'She should watch her mouth,' said Blake. 'I need that amulet, and I'm going to get it. It's my only way out of this mess. I don't want to harm you, but if she keeps pushing me, you'll both regret it.'

'Are you in trouble?' asked Holly. It dawned on her that Tony Blake's desire to find the amulet must be fuelled by more than simple greed. No sane person would behave like this unless they were being driven by something.

'Trouble?' said Blake with a bark of laughter. 'Yes. You could say I was in trouble.'

'Maybe we can help?' said Holly.

'I'll be able to help myself, once I've got my hands on that amulet,' said Blake.

'How come you're so sure it's still there?' said Tracy. 'I mean, come *on*! A few scraps of information over the telephone, a couple of whacky poems? It could all be a hoax. Then what will you do?'

'It's no hoax,' said Blake. 'I told you, I was born

in this village. I've known the stories about Oliver Duke all my life. And the story I remember best is the one about the lost amulet. The Bad Luck Duke's amulet. No one knew where he'd hidden it, but we all heard the stories about how valuable it was.' A shark-like grin spread over his pudgy features. 'And I'm going to find it.' He frowned. 'OK. Now, walk!'

'In any particular direction?' asked Tracy.

Blake cast his eyes about. '*That* way,' he said, pointing with the rifle.

'You're wrong,' said Tracy. 'The church is this way.' She nodded in another direction. Nothing but dark trees showed through the trailing curtains of snow.

Blake's eyes narrowed. He clearly didn't trust her to be telling him the truth.

'Look,' said Tracy. 'I want to get out of this as much as you do. Do you think I *like* being marched through here at gunpoint?' She stretched her arm the way she had indicated. 'See that tree with the broken branch? I saw that on the way from the church.'

Tony Blake hesitated.

'OK,' said Tracy. 'Don't believe me, then. Let's just all wander around here until we freeze to death.'

'We'll go your way,' said Blake. 'But you'd better not be trying to fool me.'

Holly glanced nervously at Tracy. Was this a trick? Did Tracy have some plan to lead Tony Blake round in circles until rescue came? Tracy gave a sly wink. Yes, that was *exactly* what she was doing.

They carried on walking through the wood. *I hope Belinda and Jamie have got to the village by now*, thought Holly. *We can't keep this up for ever.*

A dark line stretched in the distance through the trees.

'I think maybe I was wrong after all,' Tracy said quickly. 'I think we should go back.'

But it was too late. Tony Blake peered through the snow just as a flurry of wind drew the white veil aside to show the grey wall of the church, with the ghostly-looking tower seeming to hang weightlessly in the air above it.

Tracy had seen the dark line, and recognised it as the churchyard wall. She realised she'd been *too* clever. Hoping to lead Blake in the wrong direction, she had accidentally taken him in exactly the right direction.

'I think not,' said Blake. 'Keep going.'

The wasteland was a sea of snow. They left dark prints as they walked towards the solitary mass of the ancient oak tree.

'Don't move,' said Blake. He walked around the craggy tree, searching for some split or gap in the gnarled wood. Some place where a hunted man could have thrust the amulet.

'I didn't mean to lead him here,' hissed Tracy.

'I know,' whispered Holly. 'I guessed that much.'

Blake stared up into the twisted branches. About two and a half metres into the air, the trunk split into two, leaving a kind of saddle in between.

Blake motioned towards Tracy with the rifle.

'You,' he said. 'Climb up there.' He looked at Holly. 'Help her. Quick, now.'

Holly backed against the tree, cupping her hands for Tracy's foot.

'Run for it if you get the chance,' whispered Tracy as she hefted herself up. She stretched her arms around the broad trunk, resting her other foot on Holly's shoulder as she balanced herself.

The saddle between the spread of the split trunk was deep in snow. Tracy's fingers were numb and freezing as she felt through the crisp covering. She clutched at a ridge of wood and pulled herself up, getting her knee into a safe position and lifting herself up to crouch precariously in the tree.

She looked down at Blake.

'Now what?' she asked, leaning her back against a branch and tucking her hands under her arms for warmth.

'Search,' said Blake. 'There must be a hole or something. Feel around.'

Tracy frowned down at him. She wondered briefly whether she dared jump down on top of him. But he was standing watchfully a couple of metres away from the tree – as if the same thought had occurred to him.

She ploughed her hands through the snow, her nails scratching uncomfortably on the rugged bark as she cleared the area between her feet.

There *was* something. A natural groove running along the top of the saddle. She scrabbled at it, pulling out broken splinters of bark, old leaves and clods of sodden lichen. And then, as she dug her fingers deeper into the cleft, she felt something catch against her nails.

'Oh, my lord!' she gasped, clawing away the debris that clogged the split. 'It's *here*! I've *got* it!' She could see a dark brown fold of something, jammed fast into the cleft.

Blake moved closer, staring up at her, his mouth half open.

'What?' He said. 'What is it?'

'I don't know,' said Tracy. 'I can't get it out.' She worked her fingers in beside the object, trying to prise it out from underneath. It came loose so suddenly that she nearly overbalanced.

It was a brown leather pouch, hard and brittle from the years in the tree. Even as she lifted it up, the leather cracked to pieces, splintering in her fingers.

The bag was no bigger than her palm. Through the cracked leather Tracy could see a layer of coarse cloth wrapped around something hard.

'Throw it down,' said Blake, his voice hoarse with excitement. 'Throw it down and I promise I'll let you both go.'

Tracy tossed the bag down and it thudded into the snow.

Tony Blake grabbed it up, hitching the rifle under his arm as his trembling fingers picked the last of the leather away.

He hardly looked up as Tracy came slithering down out of the tree.

He pulled at the cloth and it fell to pieces in his hands.

'It is,' he breathed. 'It's the amulet!'

It was a curved disc of engraved and finely wrought blackened metal. He ran a thumb over it, wiping away the dust from the cloth.

'*Ohh!*' gasped Holly. Now that the dirt had been cleaned away she could see the jewels that encrusted the face of the amulet. A ring of white diamonds – twenty or more – glimmering in the light. And at the centre a huge, multi-faceted ruby, red as blood and as big as an acorn.

Tony Blake's hands shook as he stared down at the amulet.

'Are you going to let us go?' asked Holly.

He looked at her as if she'd woken him out of a dream. For a few moments his eyes seemed not even to see the two girls.

He pulled himself together, pushing the amulet

165

into his coat pocket and bringing the rifle down into his hands.

'I don't think so,' he said. 'I don't think that's a very good idea at all.' A new, cold light had come into his eyes as he looked from Holly to Tracy. 'In fact,' he said, 'I think you'd both better come with me. We've got quite a long journey ahead of us.'

'Wh – where are you taking us?' asked Holly.

A nasty smile flickered at the corner of his mouth.

'Somewhere where you won't be able to call the police,' he said. His voice hardened. 'Now! Both of you: Walk!'

'And then we heard a shot,' panted Belinda as she ran alongside the policeman. She was breathlessly filling him in on the day's events as they ran towards the church. 'So Holly—'

'That's my sister,' Jamie broke in.

'Yes, Jamie's sister – went to find out what had happened, while we went the other way to get help,' Belinda continued.

'And Belinda got caught on a fence,' said Jamie.

'He doesn't want to know *that*,' said Belinda, glaring round at him.

'So the last you saw of Blake was in the church?' asked the policeman.

'That's right,' said Belinda.

They came to the churchyard gate. The policeman spread his arms to stop Belinda and Jamie.

'I want you two to stay here,' he said. 'Keep well
out of sight. There will be some more men here
soon. Tell them what you told me, OK?' He gave
them a grim nod. 'Don't worry,' he said. 'We'll
soon have him sorted out.'

Belinda and Jamie watched from behind the wall
as the policeman sprinted to the side of the church.
He gave a single, cautious glance along the wall,
then ran out of sight.

'I'm not hanging about back here,' said Jamie. 'I
want to see what happens.'

'Jamie – no,' called Belinda as he ran along the
line of the policeman's footprints. 'Oh, heck!' She
followed him, her breath coming out in clouds, her
legs weak with running.

The policeman was standing at the back gate of
the churchyard wall, staring around, his truncheon
gripped firmly in his hand.

They heard him speaking into his receiver.
'No sign of him at the back of the church.
There are footprints in the snow. I'm following
them.'

A confused line of tracks showed, leading out of
the trees to one side. The continuing fall of snow
blurred the outlines, making it impossible to tell
which way the tracks were heading.

From the woods, Belinda saw the dark trail lead

to the oak tree. The policeman was following the footprints towards the edge of the woodland.

'Hey!' she shouted. '*This* way.' She ran towards the tree. The prints were jumbled and over-trodden under the tree. Sure signs of more than one person having been there.

The policeman came running towards them. 'I thought I told you—'

'Look!' Belinda pointed into the tree. The snow had been disrupted in the dip where the trunk divided, and the snow around the broad trunk was flecked with scraps and splinters of tree-mould and bark. Belinda crouched, picking up pieces of fragile brown cloth. 'They've been here already,' she said, looking up at the policeman. 'They must have found the amulet.'

'He'll go back to the van,' exclaimed Jamie. 'If he's got the amulet, he'll want to get away from here.'

'I know where the van is,' said Belinda. 'At least, I know where it *was*. Behind the pub. Behind The Duke Oliver.'

More tracks led away around the far side of the churchyard wall. Fresher tracks, less muddled by new snow. Two sets of small prints and one of larger, heavier shoes.

'That's Holly and Tracy,' said Belinda. 'It must be. He's got both of them.'

The policeman spoke into his receiver. 'The

168

suspect is thought to be heading for a van,' he said. 'Parked near The Duke Oliver. He's got two girls with him. I'm coming over.'

He turned to Belinda and Jamie. 'You two go back to the railway station,' he said.

'But we want to help,' said Jamie.

'Do as I say,' snapped the policeman. He looked sternly at Belinda. 'Just *do* it!'

Belinda grabbed Jamie's arm. 'Come on,' she said. 'Do as he says.' They watched as the policeman loped off across the wasteland.

'How are they going to stop him?' said Jamie. 'They aren't even *armed*.'

'I don't know,' said Belinda. 'Let's just get back to the railway station, shall we?'

Jamie's comment seemed all too accurate to her. How *would* they stop Blake? And more worryingly, how could they do *anything* while he was holding Holly and Tracy hostage?

'Where are you taking us?' asked Holly.

Tony Blake had marched them round the church and into the woodland that skirted the road to the railway. He was obviously taking no chances that they might be seen on the open road.

'Be quiet,' said Blake, staring through the fence that blocked their way forward. Over to the right they could see the station. He motioned them to the left along the fence.

169

'This is it,' he said. The fence was hanging off its post, curled over and bent down. 'Climb over,' he ordered.

He *knew* about this, thought Holly. Perhaps Blake had used this route before.

They clambered over the fence and came out into the open.

'Cross the line,' said Blake. 'No tricks, now. And make it snappy!'

The three of them ran across the railway tracks. Holly glanced towards the station. If only someone was looking in their direction! But the place seemed deserted. Not a single figure stood on the snow-swept platform. At that moment it felt to Holly as if they could be the only people on *earth*!

Ahead of them Holly saw the back wall of the buildings that stood alongside the railway line. Beyond another fence she saw the snow-covered open area behind The Duke Oliver. The white van was parked there again, a little distance from the pub, lying in the lee of a blank wall.

There was a break in the fence where someone had prised the wire away from a standing post. Tony Blake pushed them through.

As they approached the van, they heard the alsatian's welcoming bark.

Tony Blake fumbled in his pocket for the keys.

'I'm not getting in there with that dog,' said Tracy.

170

'You'll do as you're told,' said Blake. He opened the back doors. The dog sprang out, barking and jumping up at its master.

'Luther! In the van!' commanded Blake. But the large dog had other ideas. It had been locked alone in that van for a long time. It ran off, its tongue lolling.

'Luther!' The animal gave a single guilty look towards Tony Blake before gathering its legs under it and running along the alley.

Blake cursed, looking round at the two girls.

'Get in there,' he said.

They climbed into the back of the van and he slammed the doors closed on them. They saw him stare after the dog for a few seconds, as if debating with himself. But Blake's urge to escape must have been stronger than his desire to recapture the dog, because he went round to the front of the van and got into the driver's seat.

Holly and Tracy crouched in the back of the van. Tony Blake had the rifle across his lap. He put the key in the ignition and turned it. The motor whined.

The two girls looked at each other. That had not been the sound of a very healthy engine. Blake twisted the key and the motor let out another feeble whine.

'It won't start,' mouthed Tracy. Holly gave her a brief nod. Blake let out a series of curses and tried for a third time. This time the engine caught, coughing into life, the engine roaring as he pumped the throttle.

He looked over his shoulder, hammering the gear-stick into reverse and sending the van careering backwards towards the open ground behind the pub. The girls tumbled in the back of the van as he changed gears, spun the wheel and drove the van up the alley beside the pub. He flicked a switch and the wipers smeared the thick snow off the windscreen.

Suddenly his foot jammed down on the brake. Tracy saw a dark shape directly in front of them. It was the dog.

The van jerked to a halt, sending Tracy and Holly flying forwards against the back of the seats.

In the confusion Holly saw her chance. Both of Blake's hands were on the steering wheel. She half-fell over the back of the passenger seat, grabbing for the rifle as it lay across Blake's lap. His fingers clutched at it, but too late. With a gasp, Holly managed to shove the rifle out through the partly-opened window of the passenger door.

Blake twisted to grab her but his head snapped round as a car came speeding around the corner of the pub from the main road.

Tracy let out a yell. It was a police car.

Blake stepped down hard on the throttle, spinning the wheel as the van leaped forwards. Holly and Tracy were sent crashing into the back of the van as it swerved.

They heard a scream of metal as the side of the van scraped along the side of the police car. They were hurled sideways as Blake turned into the road, tyres screeching.

He gunned along the road. Clinging to the side of the van, Holly briefly saw through the back window that the police car was backing out of the alley.

The van swerved again, heading towards the level-crossing. Bruised and battered, Tracy caught hold of the back of a seat. Through the windscreen she saw the flashing of the level-crossing's red lights, and heard the bleeping of the warning sirens.

Blake hammered his foot down, the falling barrier of the level-crossing almost hitting the roof of the van as they sped under it.

'No!' shouted Tracy. She jumped forward, throwing her arms over Blake's face. He clawed at her arms as the van bumped over the track. They were tumbled again as the van lost power and jerked to a halt. The engine cut out.

Blake's elbow cracked back, sending Tracy catapulting over Holly. Through the chaos, the two girls heard the whine of the engine as Blake fought to get the van started again.

But above that sound, and getting rapidly louder,

was another noise. The increasing rumble and roar of an approaching train.

Blake's head turned, his eyes wide with terror.

Holly stared in absolute horror through the side window, seeing the blunt face of the oncoming train. She covered her eyes, her ears filled with the terrible blare of the train's horn as it thundered towards the stranded van.

12   Bad luck

As Belinda and Jamie ran across the railway station carpark, they saw the police car speeding off over the level-crossing.

The uniformed station manager stood at the open doors of the station.

'You'd better come in here,' he said. 'The police will find your friends, don't worry.'

They went into his office. Despite her anxiety for Holly and Tracy, Belinda felt relieved finally to be out of the snow. Both she and Jamie were soaked through and shivering with cold.

'The police already knew about Tony Blake,' said Belinda through chattering teeth. '*How* did they know?'

'More to the point,' said the station manager, 'how did you lot get involved with him?'

'It's a long story,' said Belinda, moving to stand over the electric fire, stretching her hands out towards the blessed warmth.

'Is it something to do with the amulet?' asked Jamie. 'Is that why they're after him?'

The manager looked bemused. 'I don't know about that,' he said. 'All I was told was to keep an eye open for this man.' He picked up a photocopied sheet from his desk. It showed a photograph of Tony Blake. Beneath the photo was some writing: details of the white van and some information about Blake himself.

'What has he done?' asked Belinda.

'It's fraud of some kind,' said the manager. 'Apparently he works for a firm of surveyors —'

'We know that,' said Jamie. 'Gardener, Preston and Blake. They're doing some work at our house in Willow Dale.'

'Well,' continued the manager, 'it seems that their annual accounts audit threw up some financial chicanery. Your Mr Blake has been writing himself some large cheques – using the firm's money to buy himself a nice big house. He must have got wind that they'd rumbled him, because he vanished a couple of days ago, just before they called in the police.'

'*That* explains why he was so dead-set on getting his hands on that amulet,' said Belinda, looking at Jamie. 'I expect he planned on disappearing permanently on the proceeds.'

'This amulet you keep talking about,' said the manager. 'What is it, exactly?'

'Hidden highwayman's treasure,' said Jamie. 'We've been following clues, and —' The ringing of a bell interrupted him.

'Sorry,' said the manager. 'I shan't be a minute. There's a train approaching.'

He went out on to the platform.

A few seconds later they heard him shouting. Belinda ran to the door, hoping that it was something to do with the capture of Tony Blake.

The manager was running along the platform, waving his arms and shouting. It only took Belinda an instant to see what the trouble was.

She let out a gasp of shock. Through the steadily falling snow she could see Tony Blake's white van halted across the tracks in the middle of the level-crossing. And bearing down on it around the long curve of the railway line was the train.

She ran on to the platform, her hands over her mouth as the bellow of the train's horn blasted above the clatter of wheels.

Holly screamed, her voice echoed by the screech of the train's brakes as the driver fought to bring the onrushing monster to a halt.

Seeing their peril, Tracy clambered to the rear of the van, kicking at the locked doors, hoping against hope that she would be able to force them open.

His face a mask of desperation, Tony Blake snatched at the ignition key and jerked his foot up and down on the throttle.

The train was slowing, sparks flying up from the wheels. For a moment, Holly saw the shock on the train driver's face before the van gave a sudden lurch and sprang forwards.

There was a horrendous bang and Holly was flung like a rag doll across the van as it skewed round and tipped on to its side.

She covered her head with her arms, almost deafened by the howl of tortured metal and by the roar of the train, as she tensed herself for the final deadly impact.

But it never came. The noise ebbed away to a pulsing silence. She opened her eyes. The van was on its side, but it was still whole. One of the back doors was hanging open. Before she had time to gather her wits, she felt Tracy's hand on her arm and she was pulled out into the open.

She was dizzied and battered, but by some miracle they had survived. The two girls staggered to their feet. A rear corner of the van was caved in where the train had hit it. It *was* a miracle! Tony Blake's final desperate effort had jolted the van almost clear of the track. The slowing train had clipped the back of the van, spinning it over as it swept past.

The two girls stumbled away from the crossing. Shocked faces stared down at them from the carriages that reared above them. Too relieved for words, Holly and Tracy fell into each other's arms as figures came running towards them through the snow.

* * *

'I'm glad I didn't realise you two were *in* the van,' said Belinda, shaking her head. 'I'd have just *died*!'

'*We* very nearly did,' said Tracy. 'I never want as close a call as *that* again.'

Holly nodded her profound agreement.

They were in the station manager's office, wrapped in blankets and drinking mugs of hot, steaming tea.

It had taken a few minutes to drag Tony Blake out of the van. He had hit his head in the crash and had been carried somewhere dry while somebody called for an ambulance.

Meanwhile, the girls were taken to the station to be reunited with Belinda and Jamie and to explain everything to the astonished policeman.

The train had clattered the few remaining metres to the platform and the shocked passengers were standing about waiting to be told what to do next.

The manager was on the phone, his voice urgent as he contacted his superiors to tell them what had happened.

Another policeman came into the office.

'Is Mr Blake all right?' asked Holly.

'He'll survive,' said the policeman. 'He's lucky to be alive, pulling a stunt like that.' He opened his hand. 'I found this on him.' It was the amulet.

'*That's* what this was all about,' said Tracy. 'The Bad Luck Duke's amulet!'

'Bad luck for Blake,' said Belinda, gazing at the disc of blackened metal with its glinting jewels. 'What on earth must it be worth?'

'Thousands of pounds,' breathed Jamie. '*Millions* of pounds!'

'Excuse me.' A woman stood at the office door. 'I realise you're busy, but can someone help me, please?'

They looked round at her. She was in her thirties with short black hair; a puzzled expression on her thin face.

'I don't know this area,' she said.

A light went on in Holly's head. The woman's voice. She recognised that voice.

'We'll get the train running again as soon as we can, madam,' said the manager. 'If you could just be patient for a short while.'

'No, it's not that,' said the woman. 'I wanted this stop anyway. I just wondered if anyone could direct me to Gilchrist's bookshop.'

Holly's mouth fell open. She glanced at the wall clock. It was a few minutes before four o'clock.

'Are you Tessa?' breathed Holly, gazing at the woman.

The woman gave her a startled look. 'My name's Tessa Parson, yes,' she said. 'But how—'

'Tessa?' gasped Belinda. 'The Tessa who's looking for the Bad Luck Duke's amulet?'

180

Tessa Parson's face changed to a look of pure astonishment. 'How do you know about that?'

'That's kind of a long story,' said Tracy. 'But I think that guy has what you're looking for.'

Tessa's eyes almost stood clear of her head as she saw the amulet in the policeman's hand.

'Will someone tell me what this is all about?' asked the first policeman.

Holly managed to do most of the explaining, her narrative interrupted frequently by Jamie and the other girls, as Tessa Parson, the two policemen and the station manager listened in growing amazement.

'All we *don't* understand,' finished Holly, and looking at Tessa, 'is how *you* knew about the amulet.'

'It's simple,' said Tessa. 'I'm a direct descendant of the daughter of the man everyone knows as the Bad Luck Duke.'

'Of his *daughter*!' exclaimed Belinda. 'The daughter who vanished after he was executed. The person he wrote the poems for!'

'That's right,' said Tessa Parson. 'I was tracing my ancestry through the county records. I got right back to the early eighteenth century – which was when I came up with the name of Elizabeth Duke. I had a friend who was an expert in these things.' She frowned at the girls. 'It was him that I was phoning when you heard me. We've been doing

181

a lot of research together. That was how we came upon the story of the Bad Luck Duke – and of the lost amulet and the fact that Oliver Duke had left some clues for his daughter in a poem. It took us some time to unravel it all, but we finally found out about the book.' She smiled. 'That was where we came to a halt. We couldn't find a copy of the book anywhere.'

'That's hardly surprising,' said Belinda. 'The man in the shop said there were probably only a handful ever printed.'

'I know,' said Tessa. 'It was a private printing. I searched for days through the records of a specialist shop in Brompton before I found out that there was a bookshop in Lychthorpe that might have a copy.'

'You'd have saved us an awful lot of chasing around if you'd come straight over and picked it up,' said Tracy with a grin.

'I couldn't get away,' said Tessa. She gazed again at the amulet. 'Can I hold it?' she asked the policeman. 'Just for a few minutes. I've been waiting for this moment for such a long time.'

The policeman rested the amulet across her open palms.

'Do we get a reward for finding it?' asked Jamie. Holly kicked his ankle. 'Ow! What was that for?' he yelled.

'For being greedy!' said Holly.

'But we *found* it,' said Jamie.

'I'm afraid this counts as treasure trove,' said the first policeman.

'What does that mean?' asked Tracy.

'I know what it means,' said Belinda. 'Treasure trove is stuff that has been deliberately hidden, isn't it?' she said, looking up at the policeman.

'I'm afraid so,' he said. 'And treasure trove is the property of the state.'

Jamie's face fell.

'But there *might* be a reward,' said the policeman, rubbing his chin. 'The question is: who should it go to?'

'Us?' said Jamie dubiously. He looked around at the others. He shook his head sadly. 'Not us,' he said. He looked at the amulet with a sigh, dreams of truck-loads of computer games fading before his eyes. He looked at Tessa.

'If there's any reward, I suppose it should go to you,' he said.

Holly put her arm around his shoulders.

'I'm being very brave about this,' he said gloomily. 'I hope everyone is taking note.'

'If there is a reward,' said Tessa, 'I'm going to donate it to my local museum.' She looked up at the policeman. 'What happens next?' she asked.

'I think we'd better get down to the police station for a few statements,' he said. He looked at Jamie and the girls. 'But first of all, I think we'd better telephone your parents so they can come and collect you. They'll want to know what you've been up to.'

'I bet they will,' said Belinda. She grinned at the others. '*Another* lot of explaining to do,' she said.

Jamie and the girls stood waiting in the railway station carpark for the police car to come for them. Tessa Parson and the policeman stood nearby.

The snow was easing off and the sky was beginning to darken towards evening. It felt to Holly like it had been a very long day.

'Holly?' said Jamie. 'Just one thing.'

'What's that?'

'When you start boasting about how the Mystery Club found that amulet, you *will* explain that the three of you couldn't have done *anything* without *me*, won't you?' he said.

'What do you want?' said Tracy. 'A medal?'

He looked affrontedly at her. 'Who started all this?' he said. 'You three wouldn't have done a *thing* if it wasn't for me. *And* I got a black eye. I don't see anyone else with any black eyes.'

'Why, you little monster!' exclaimed Holly. 'Do you really expect to be *thanked* for getting us into all this? If I had my way, you'd be given a pair of concrete boots and dumped in the canal!'

'No,' said Belinda, coming up behind Jamie. 'Be fair – he does deserve *something* for all his effort.'

Jamie beamed, not noticing Belinda wink at her two friends.

'See?' he said, grinning. 'Even Belinda thinks – *ummph!*' His voice was cut off as Belinda crammed a huge snowball into his face.

'That's for eavesdropping in the first place!' she said, as Tracy and Holly laughed. Jamie squirmed as she hooked open the back of his coat and stuffed another snowball down the back of his neck. 'And that's for all your wisecracks about my weight!'

'Way to go!' laughed Tracy, scooping up a handful of snow and launching it at Jamie. 'That's for getting us chased by a crazy man!'

Holly rocked with laughter as Jamie tottered under the rain of snowballs. 'And *this*,' she said, swiping up more snow to throw at her brother, 'is for thinking you can tangle with the Mystery Club and get away with it!'

The laughter of the three girls echoed around the carpark as they ran after the fleeing Jamie, pelting him with snowballs.

It was a sadder, wetter and wiser Jamie who sat in the police station later that evening waiting with the others for his parents to arrive.

'What in heaven's name have you got this boy involved in?' asked Mrs Adams, looking from Jamie to Holly.

Holly shook her head. 'I knew it,' she sighed,

looking across at Tracy and Belinda. 'I just *knew* I'd get the blame.'

'Well?' said Mrs Adams. 'I'm waiting.'

Holly took a deep breath. 'It's a long story,' she said. 'And *this* time, it really *isn't* my fault!'

DARK HORSE

by Fiona Kelly

Holly, Belinda and Tracy are back in the
eleventh thrilling adventure in the
Mystery Club series, published by
Hodder Children's Books.

Turn the page to read the first chapter . . .

1   A mysterious call

'I'm afraid Belinda's gone out. She's riding Melt-down up to the riding centre to get her entry forms for the showjumping competition next week.'

Mrs Hayes was just getting into her sports car as Holly arrived at her friend's luxurious, chalet-style house in the executive part of Willow Dale.

'Thanks, Mrs Hayes. I'll go and find her.' Holly's grey eyes sparkled as she gave her friend's mother a bright smile.

'I'm just off to the hairdresser,' said Mrs Hayes.

Holly thought Belinda's glamorous mother looked as if she'd just emerged *from* the salon. As always she looked immaculate. Not a single hair was out of place.

A soft breeze ruffled Holly's light brown hair as she stood and watched Mrs Hayes check her make-up in the car mirror, then roar off down the long, gravel drive.

Holly turned her bike round and shot off after her. She'd only called at the house on the off chance. Things seem to have gone mad at home.

Her mum's plan to take a week off from her bank manager's job to decorate the hall hadn't been a great idea. Rolls of wallpaper and ladders were all over the place, and when Jamie stepped into the bucket of paste Holly reckoned it was time to disappear.

Holly took the road that led up to the Willow Dale Riding Centre. Belinda would be surprised to see her. They hadn't planned to see each other until later, when they'd arranged to meet Tracy at the ice-cream parlour in town.

Below, Willow Dale was spread out like a map. Holly could see the church spire, the place where the old and new parts of the town met and the distant sprawl of the out-of-town shopping centre and sports complex. It was great living in a place like this; so different from her old home in London where traffic roared day and night and the air wasn't nearly so clean and fresh.

In the distance, Holly could see a horse and rider coming along the road. *That could be Belinda*, Holly thought. She stood on the pedals and waved madly. 'Hi', she shouted.

Horse and rider trotted briskly towards her.

But to Holly's embarrassment, it wasn't Belinda at all. It was a young woman in her early twenties.

'Morning!' she called. 'Is something wrong?'

Holly gulped. 'Oh, sorry. I thought you were someone else.'

She felt a bit foolish, yelling like that at a perfect stranger. Trouble was, all chestnut thoroughbreds looked alike to Holly.

'Your horse looks just like hers,' she said. 'Sorry.'

'That's OK,' the young woman replied with a smile.

It was really pretty obvious it wasn't Belinda. The rider was much slimmer and had very short black hair beneath her riding hat.

'This is Roddy,' she explained, giving her horse a pat. 'And I'm Jenny Maylam. We live at Snowdrop Farm. It's down in the valley the other side of the hill.'

'He's a great looking horse,' said Holly, although she wasn't really into horses.

'Do you live around here?' Jenny Maylam asked Holly.

'I live in the town,' Holly told her. 'I'm on my way to the riding centre to find my friend, Belinda.'

'Well, good luck,' the young woman called cheerily. 'Nice to have met you.' She dug her heels in the horse's flanks and trotted smartly off.

'Bye!' Holly called, pedalling off in the opposite direction.

At the top of the hill, Holly stopped to take a breath. Down in the valley, she could see Snowdrop Farm. A grey horse was just being loaded into a blue cattle truck. The driver put up the tail-gate then got into the cab. From a side road, a green jeep emerged. It waited while the truck pulled out into the road. The truck driver leaned from his cab to say something to the driver of the jeep. Then they parted, both going off in opposite directions.

The truck trundled up the hill towards Holly. She waited on the verge to let it pass. The driver stared at her but ignored her smile. He pulled his tweed cap down over his eyes and roared off down the road.

'That's not very friendly,' Holly muttered to herself, her eyebrows meeting in a frown.

She turned to see the truck branch off where the lane forked. She noticed it was covered in mud as if it had been driving across a field.

At the riding centre, there was no sign of Belinda, although Meltdown was tethered near the horse trough. The green jeep was parked in one of the barns.

The centre's owner, Jake Barratt, a middle-aged man in jodhpurs and a maroon sweat-shirt was shouting instructions to a group of youngsters having a riding lesson.

Holly went up to a fair-haired girl who was mucking out the stables.

'Hi, have you seen a girl in a faded green sweat-shirt and glasses?' she asked.

'Is she the one who owns that thoroughbred?' The girl indicated Meltdown, his chestnut coat gleaming in the sun. 'She was asking about entry forms for the show.'

'That's the one,' said Holly.

The girl introduced herself as Melanie Brookes. 'We've been admiring her horse,' she said. 'He's fabulous.'

'You'll be Belinda's friend for ever if she hears you say that,' Holly said. 'Meltdown's the love of her life. Any idea where she is?'

'She's gone into the office with Grant D'Angelo. He's Jake's assistant. He's organising the show.'

'Thanks,' said Holly. 'I'll go and find her.'

She was just about to bound up the steps to the office when there was a cry and a mad clatter of hooves on concrete.

A riderless grey pony suddenly came galloping wildly through the gate. Like lightning, Holly dived forward, grabbing the reins. The pony skidded to a halt, rearing up. The reins were almost torn from Holly's hand. She hung on tight, barely managing to dodge the flying hooves.

At last the pony settled on all fours and stood there trembling.

'Steady, boy!' Holly said breathlessly.

Suddenly a woman rushed through the gate looking distraught.

'Someone come quickly, Kelly's been thrown off!' she cried.

Belinda and a good-looking young man with

dark, curly hair and broad shoulders came rushing out of the office. Holly recognised him as the driver of the jeep.

There was a surprised look on Belinda's round face when she saw Holly grimly hanging on to the runaway pony.

'What are you doing here?' Belinda blurted, brushing back a stray lock of straggly brown hair. 'I thought we weren't meeting until this afternoon.'

'Where is she?' the young man was saying urgently to the woman.

'Just down the road,' she gasped.

Holly thrust the reins into Belinda's hands. 'I'll tell you in a minute!'

She bounded up the steps and into the office. Trying to keep cool, she quickly dialled 999. She tapped her foot impatiently as she heard the number ringing at the other end.

'Emergency, which service please?' The operator's voice sounded calm and unruffled.

'Ambulance, please,' Holly said quickly.

The switchboard answered immediately and Holly swiftly told them about the accident and gave the address.

Heart thudding, she ran back out. 'The ambulance is on its way!'

In the road, the young man, whom Holly had realised was Grant D'Angelo, was kneeling beside the small girl lying unconscious on the grass verge. Kelly's mother was crying and wringing her hands.

Holly told Grant what she had done.

Grant threw her a grateful glance. 'Brilliant. Well done!'

Belinda reassured the child's mother. 'The ambulance won't be long, I'm sure.' She pushed her wire-framed spectacles back on her nose.

Grant covered Kelly with his jacket. 'We mustn't move her.'

He lifted her hand gently and felt for her pulse. A frown crossed his dark brow. He stood up and put his arm round her mother's shoulders.

'I'm sure she'll be OK, Mrs Harris. Her pulse feels quite steady,' he said reassuringly.

The woman leaned against him. 'Here,' he said kindly. 'Sit down on the verge.'

Belinda sat beside Mrs Harris. 'Try not to worry,' she said. 'I've fallen off loads of times.'

Holly looked at the child's pale face beneath her black riding hat. She glanced at Grant. He shrugged, then took her arm and led her a little way away.

'I don't like it one bit,' he whispered. 'I fibbed to her mum. I didn't want her to panic but the kid's pulse is very weak. I hope the ambulance gets a move on.'

Just then, the sound of a siren came echoing towards them. Holly heaved a sigh. The sooner the little girl was in hospital, the better.

The ambulance screeched to a halt. Two paramedics jumped from the back.

Jake Barratt had run from the yard when he heard the commotion. He stood with the others as Kelly was carefully lifted on to a stretcher and borne away to the local casualty department.

Grant bit his lip. 'I hope she's not badly hurt.' He turned to Holly and Belinda. 'You feel pretty helpless in a situation like that, don't you?'

'You were brilliant,' said Belinda. 'No one could have done any more than you did.'

'He's always great with kids,' Melanie said. She gave Grant an admiring glance.

Grant shrugged and ran his hand through his dark curls. 'I just like kids, that's all.' He smiled. 'Almost as much as I like horses.' He turned to Holly. 'Are you riding in the show too?'

'No, not me,' said Holly.

Belinda introduced her. 'She'll just come to cheer me on,' she said with a grin. 'What else are friends for?'

By now, Jake had gone back into the office. He poked his head round the door. 'Phone call for you, Grant!'

Grant pressed his lips together and frowned. 'Who is it?' he asked.

Jake shrugged. 'It sounds like the same man who's rung before.'

'Could you tell him I'm not here?'

Jake looked annoyed. 'Grant, this is the third time this has happened. For goodness sake, speak to the man. Maybe then he'll stop pestering you.'

Grant sighed. 'OK.' He disappeared into the office.

'By the way, Belinda,' said Jake. 'Could you tell your mum we collected some jumble for her sale and I left it in your garage yesterday. She may have already found it.'

'No problem,' said Belinda.

Belinda's mother was heavily into raising money for charity. Her latest project was organising a rummage sale in the church hall.

'Well,' said Belinda to Holly when Jake had gone, 'what *are* you doing here?'

'Things are mad at home,' Holly explained. 'I needed a break.'

Belinda pulled Meltdown's reins over his head and mounted. She patted the pocket of her faded green sweat-shirt.

'I've got the entry form,' she said. 'Grant's done me a favour and let me enter the showjumping, even though the closing date for entries was yesterday.' She groaned. 'It must be way past lunch-time. My stomach's rumbling like a train. I can feel a desire for egg and chips coming on.'

Holly grinned. Belinda was *always* hungry.

She grabbed her bike. 'Come on then, I'll race you home.'

'If I've got the energy,' Belinda sighed.

Just then, Grant came hurtling out of the office with a face like thunder.

'Get all those stables mucked out,' he shouted at a group of girls still discussing the accident. 'It's my day off tomorrow and I want to see it all done before I come back.'

He ran across the yard and jumped into his jeep. The wheels spun as he roared out of the yard and down the drive. Meltdown whinneyed in alarm.

'Whoa, boy!' said Belinda, gathering up the reins. She frowned. 'I wonder what's eating him?'

Melanie shrugged. 'He's been having an awful lot of hassle lately,' she said worriedly.

'What about?' asked Belinda.

Melanie shook her head. 'It's a real mystery actually,' she said in a low voice. 'Grant's usually really good-tempered, but since he started getting these phone calls he's been going around like a bear with a sore head.'

At the sound of the word 'mystery', Holly's ears pricked up. She looked at Belinda with a gleam in her eye.

Belinda put her hands on her hips. 'Holly, you've got that look again.'

'What look?' Holly said innocently.

'You know,' said Belinda. 'Your "come on, let's find out what's going on" expression.'

'Well,' said Holly, grinning. 'Let's do just that then, shall we?'

Belinda shook her head. 'The things you get me into!'

Another exciting mystery for The Mystery Club

DEADLY GAMES

Fiona Kelly

'Kidnapped!' Steffie exclaimed. 'Of course my brother hasn't been kidnapped! He's on a tiny island somewhere, that's all! He chose to go there,' Steffie insisted. 'There's no mystery here!'

Why is Steffie Smith behaving so strangely? She refuses to talk, but the Mystery Club – Holly, Belinda and Tracy – aren't easily deterred. And soon they're dragged into a murky world of kidnap, espionage – and even murder . . .

h HODDER

Another exciting mystery for The Mystery Club

HIDE AND SEEK

Fiona Kelly

Just as Holly was about to follow Miranda off the tube train, she suddenly felt someone wrench the plastic bag out of her hand. 'The bag!' she gasped. 'Someone's stolen it!'

A wall of people blocked the train doors and Holly had to wedge her way back into the carriage but, before Miranda could get a foothold, the doors shut and the train pulled off into a tunnel. Holly was on her own . . .

A trip to London to stay with an old friend plunges the Mystery Cub into a perplexing and frightening mystery, when a simple evening's baby-sitting turns dangerous.

TITLES AVAILABLE IN THE MYSTERY
CLUB SERIES

All these books are available at your local bookshop or newsagent, or can be ordered direct from the publisher. Just tick the titles you want and fill in the form below.

Prices and availability subject to change without notice.

Hodder & Stoughton Paperbacks, P.O. Box 11, Falmouth, Cornwall.

Please send cheque or postal order for the value of the book, and add the following for postage and packing:

U.K. including B.F.P.O. – £1.00 for one book, plus 50p for the second book, and 30p for each additional book ordered up to a £3.00 maximum.

OVERSEAS INCLUDING EIRE – £2.00 for the first book, plus £1.00 for the second book, and 50p for each additional book ordered.

OR Please debit this amount from my Access/Visa Card (delete as appropriate).

Card Number ☐☐☐☐☐☐☐☐☐☐☐☐☐☐☐☐

Amount £ ....

Expiry Date ....

Signed ....

Name ....

Address ....